The Joker's Revenge

Nancy was eager to report what she had discovered—that someone inside the store had to be involved in the pranks. She stepped onto the escalator.

All at once Nancy became aware that the escalator was picking up speed—it was going faster and faster! She whizzed past mirrors and hanging plants, all going by in a blur. Ahead of her she saw an enormous marble pillar just beyond the escalator landing.

Nancy tried to brace herself as she neared the top. She'd have to jump clear at just the right moment in order to avoid being hurt.

Suddenly the escalator jerked to a stop, catching Nancy off guard and hurling her straight toward the marble pillar!

Nancy Drew
Mystery Stories

Available from MINSTREL Books

NANCY DREW MYSTERY STORIES ®

NANCY DREW ®

THE JOKER'S REVENGE

CAROLYN KEENE

A MINSTREL® BOOK

PUBLISHED BY POCKET BOOKS

New York   London   Toronto   Sydney   Tokyo

A MINSTREL PAPERBACK *ORIGINAL*

A Minstrel Book published by
POCKET BOOKS, a division of Simon & Schuster Inc.
1230 Avenue of the Americas, New York, N.Y. 10020

Copyright © 1988 by Simon & Schuster Inc.
Cover artwork copyright © 1988 by Bob Berran
Produced by Mega-Books of New York, Inc.

ISBN: 0-671-63414-3

First Minstrel Books printing July, 1988

10 9 8 7 6 5 4 3 2 1

NANCY DREW, NANCY DREW MYSTERY STORIES, A MINSTREL BOOK and colophon are registered trademarks of Simon & Schuster Inc.

Printed in the U.S.A.

Contents

THE JOKER'S
REVENGE

1

A Strange Deck of Cards

"Well, here it is," George Fayne announced, looking up at the entrance to the large white building. "Danner and Bishop, the department store that has everything you ever wanted to buy."

"This is one time I'm going to love working on a mystery with you, Nancy," Bess Marvin said, throwing her arm around her friend's shoulder.

Nancy Drew laughed. "You mean you're going to love exploring this store and being near all those fantastic clothes!"

"You're right," Bess admitted cheerfully. "And don't leave out the part about staying at the Fitzhughs' mansion while we're in Chicago. This is going to be great!"

"Is this the same Bess who's terrified of danger on every case?" George teased.

George and Bess were first cousins and totally different types. Brown-haired, brown-eyed George was tall, slim, and athletic. Bess was short and slightly plump, with long blond hair and light blue eyes.

"Danger?" Bess repeated, staring wide-eyed at George. "Don't be silly. How could there possibly be any danger in a fabulous store like Danner and Bishop?"

"I hate to say it, Bess, but it is possible." Nancy looked at her friends, a serious expression in her blue eyes. "Mr. Fitzhugh wouldn't have called my father and asked us to come here if there weren't some sort of trouble."

Nancy's father, Carson Drew, was a well-known lawyer who had clients all over the country. He had represented Carlin Fitzhugh, the owner of Danner and Bishop, for many years.

Nancy stared up past the polished stone steps that led to the oversize revolving door. Huge marble columns flanked the entrance to the store. She had to admit that Bess had a point. Danner and Bishop was the largest, most popular store in Chicago. It seemed an unlikely place for a dangerous adventure.

The wind off Lake Michigan whipped around the girls. Bess shivered and clutched the collar of her coat tightly around her neck. "It's really cold here. Can we go inside now?"

"Sure." Nancy brushed a lock of her reddish blond hair away from her face. "Let's go!"

The girls headed up the steps and pushed through the revolving door. Inside, they were surrounded by warmth and gentle music and felt deep, lush carpeting beneath their feet.

Bess sighed happily. "I love this place. It's so much better than any store in River Heights."

"It sure is," Nancy agreed absently as she looked around. Spotting an information desk, she motioned for her friends to follow her. "Mr. Fitzhugh said to find the store manager, Bennett Lloyd, as soon as we got here," she told Bess and George.

The woman at the information desk smiled at the girls in a friendly way. When Nancy asked her where they could find Bennett Lloyd, she pointed out a small, thin man in a well-cut dark suit. He was rearranging a display of men's hats and scarves. Nancy thanked the woman and approached the store manager.

"Mr. Lloyd?"

"Yes?" The man spun around and looked at Nancy through old-fashioned horn-rimmed glasses. "What can I do for you?"

"I'm Nancy Drew from River Heights," she said, extending her hand. "And these are my friends George Fayne and Bess Marvin. Mr. Fitzhugh told us to look for you when we arrived."

"Oh, yes," Mr. Lloyd said, shaking each girl's hand briefly. "Mr. Fitzhugh told me to expect you. He asked me to take you up to his office as soon as you arrived." Bennett Lloyd smiled at the girls. "Will you please follow me to the back of the store? We'll take the employees' elevator."

"I could spend all of my money right here," Bess declared as they walked past long glass counters displaying a large array of cosmetics. "If I ever win the lottery, I'll bring all my millions to Danner and Bishop."

"And blow every cent on makeup and perfume?" George asked, shaking her head.

"Of course not," Bess said airily. "I'd need dresses, furs, jewels . . ."

Nancy wasn't paying much attention to her friends' joking. She was scanning the store, trying to spot anything that might give her a clue to the mystery Mr. Fitzhugh had asked her to solve. But all she saw were salespeople waiting on customers or fixing up displays. Nothing seemed to be out of the ordinary.

The store was beautiful. Nancy noticed that the walls were painted in pastel colors and were covered with gleaming mirrors. The soft lighting shone on the merchandise displays. Even the salespeople seemed to have a polished look. They appeared efficient and very much in control.

The elevator stopped at the fourth floor. "This way, ladies," Mr. Lloyd announced, leading Nancy, Bess, and George down a wide hallway.

At the end of the hall, Mr. Lloyd approached a woman sitting at a desk in front of a huge double door made of dark carved mahogany. He cleared his throat and said, "Ms. Drew and her friends are here to see Mr. Fitzhugh, Grace."

The woman smiled pleasantly at the girls. "Mr. Fitzhugh has been expecting you. You can go right in."

Bennett Lloyd hesitated, then pulled the heavy door open.

"Mr. Fitzhugh, I'd like you to meet Nancy Drew, Bess Marvin, and George Fayne," Mr. Lloyd announced.

"Delighted to meet you!" a hearty voice thundered. A short, stocky man stood up behind a gigantic desk. He rounded the desk and came striding toward the girls. At first sight of Carlin Fitzhugh's ruddy face and his shock of silver-white hair, Nancy knew that he was a distinguished and important man.

"Welcome to the Danner and Bishop team," the store owner boomed. He grasped Nancy's hand and started pumping it up and down in a firm handshake. "I've heard a lot about you,

Nancy. Your father has told me a great deal about the many cases you've solved. That's why I've asked you to come spend some time here at the store."

"I'm happy to finally meet you, Mr. Fitzhugh," Nancy replied. "I've been wondering about this mystery you want us to help you solve."

"Well, then, let's get right down to business, shall we?" Mr. Fitzhugh motioned to three soft leather chairs arranged around his desk. "Make yourselves comfortable."

As the girls moved farther into the room and sat down, Nancy noticed that Bennett Lloyd stayed close to the door, shifting his weight back and forth from one foot to the other.

Carlin Fitzhugh went back to his desk and sat down. He leaned forward and looked at the girls. "For the past two weeks, someone has been playing practical jokes on the customers and staff of the store." He opened one of the desk drawers and pulled out a stack of what looked like large playing cards. He handed them to Nancy, who flipped through them quickly.

"Jokers," she said. "They're all the same." Nancy looked up at Mr. Fitzhugh.

"Yes," Carlin Fitzhugh said, nodding. "They're our only clue to the person who is playing the pranks. Every time one of the pranks happens, a card like this is left at the scene."

"What kind of pranks are they?" Nancy asked.

"They were harmless enough—at first," replied Fitzhugh. "Whoopee cushions in the ladies' lounge, all of the appliances in the housewares department turning on at once, that sort of thing—"

"Pardon me for interrupting." A pretty blond woman in her twenties entered the office. She was dressed in a very stylish navy blue business suit.

"Girls, I'd like you to meet my daughter, Ann," Carlin Fitzhugh said proudly. "Ann recently graduated from business school and is working here at the store now. Someday she'll take my place and run the whole organization. I believe in having a family operation," he added. "Annie, I'd like you to meet Nancy Drew and her friends Bess Marvin and George Fayne."

"I'm pleased to meet you," Ann said. "I hope you'll be able to help us put a stop to all this."

"There are a lot of cards," George observed. "That's an awful lot of pranks."

"Yes, the whole situation is getting out of hand," Ann Fitzhugh said. "That's why Dad thought it would be a good idea to have you start looking into this now, before any more damage is done to our business."

"I can't believe that practical jokes could seriously harm a store like Danner and Bishop," Bess said, frowning.

"They can," Carlin Fitzhugh said. "The

pranks have hurt our reputation. The whoopee cushions didn't win us any friends, I can assure you. One time the price tags on several pieces of expensive merchandise were switched around. We tried to explain to the customers what had happened, but when they complained we had to sell the items at greatly reduced prices."

"Don't forget the leaking pens in the stationery department," Bennett Lloyd put in. "What a mess that was."

"Yes," Carlin Fitzhugh agreed. "A lot of customers had something to say about that! We had to foot the cleaning bills for all the stained clothes, handbags, and briefcases. And that's not all. I'm afraid we're losing some long-standing customers who are now going across town to Paley's, our rival department store.

"The list of pranks goes on and on," Mr. Fitzhugh said. "But until last Saturday, they were just annoying—not dangerous."

"What happened on Saturday?" Nancy wanted to know.

"A chandelier in the ladies' sportswear department crashed to the floor," said Ann.

"Oh no!" gasped Bess. "Was anyone hurt?"

"Fortunately, no," Carlin Fitzhugh replied grimly. "But it was a very close call." He turned to Nancy. "We discovered that the support chain had been cut. So you can see why we were so anxious to have you investigate."

"Have you called the police about the pranks?" Nancy asked.

Mr. Fitzhugh shook his head. "If we notified the police, the newspapers would get hold of the story. That would bring even more bad publicity to Danner and Bishop. We're in enough trouble with our customers already!"

Nancy nodded. Then she looked down at the strange oversize cards in her hand. The joker on each card was wearing a multicolored jester's outfit. On each joker's face was a twisted, sneering smile. The staring eyes had an evil expression in them.

Bess shuddered as she peered over Nancy's shoulder. "That face is enough to give a person nightmares!"

Nancy noticed that every one of the cards was signed in green pen across the bottom. The signature read, "The Joker."

"I'm sorry," said Mr. Fitzhugh. "I know these cards don't give you much to go on."

"Do you have any suspects in mind? Anybody whose behavior has been unusual lately?" Nancy asked.

"No," Mr. Fitzhugh said. "That's what makes this so frustrating. We have no ideas at all."

"If you ask me," Bennett Lloyd broke in, "the culprit isn't anyone inside the store. We have a very loyal staff here at Danner and Bishop. It must be someone from the outside."

9

"Well, that's what Nancy is here to find out." Carlin Fitzhugh waved an impatient hand.

"Did you check these cards for fingerprints?" Nancy asked.

"Yes," Ann replied. "We had our security staff check that. They say the person who handled the cards must have been wearing gloves."

"I'd like to keep some of these cards," Nancy said.

"Of course," Mr. Fitzhugh said. He took the rest of the cards back from Nancy and carefully tucked them into the top drawer of his desk. "I thought that the best plan of action would be to place you girls undercover, working in the store. That's why I asked you to bring your friends, Nancy. The more people we have looking for this practical joker, the more effective we can be."

"That sounds like a good idea," Nancy said. Bess and George nodded their heads in agreement.

"Fine. We've tried to pick jobs that will allow you to move around the store a lot. George, I'd like you to work with the maintenance staff."

"That's all right with me," George said.

Ann smiled. "And Nancy, we thought the best job for you would be as a guard on our security force."

"Great," Nancy said. "George and I should be able to cover the whole store this way."

"What about me?" Bess asked shyly. "Maybe I

10

could do something in sales, like in the shoe department."

George rolled her eyes. "Somehow I just *knew* Bess would want to work in the shoe department!"

Bess's face reddened as her friends laughed. "She probably has more than fifty pairs in her closet at home!" George added.

"Well, then I think the shoe department is just the place for you, Bess," Ann said, laughing along with the girls. "The department is located in the middle of the store in a very busy section. You'll be able to see a lot from your post. And, as a matter of fact, we desperately need another salesperson there!"

"I think it would be best if no one, not even your department supervisors, knew about your undercover work," Mr. Fitzhugh said to the girls. "You'll report back to Ann or myself about what you learn. And Mr. Lloyd will be happy to assist you in any way he can, won't you, Bennett?"

"Yes, yes, of course," Mr. Lloyd replied.

"I hope this mystery is solved quickly, Nancy." Carlin Fitzhugh came around to the front of his desk. "Danner and Bishop was just a third-rate store when I took over. I've spent years building it into the top store in Chicago. I'm planning to pass Danner and Bishop on to my family, and I'd hate to see its reputation totally ruined because of these silly pranks."

"Don't worry, Mr. Fitzhugh," George said. "Nancy will put the practical joker out of action."

"I'll do my best," replied Nancy. "But our joker has been very clever. He or she has been able to pull these pranks without being seen. And the incident last Saturday proves that these aren't just silly pranks anymore."

"What are you getting at, Nancy?" demanded Carlin Fitzhugh.

Nancy looked at him. "As you said, Mr. Fitzhugh, no one was hurt by that falling chandelier. But the next time, someone may not be so lucky!"

2

A Close Call

There was an uneasy silence in the room. Then Mr. Fitzhugh said quietly, "The reputation of the store is very important to me. But if anyone becomes injured by these pranks, I'll never forgive myself."

"We'll just have to make sure no one *does* get hurt," Nancy said with grim determination. "So, the sooner we catch this joker, the better." She turned to Bennett Lloyd. "Mr. Lloyd, would you get us started with our 'jobs' now?"

Mr. Lloyd nodded. Then he ushered the three girls out of Carlin Fitzhugh's office.

"I'll take you two to the personnel office," Mr. Lloyd told George and Bess as they headed down the hall. "Going through the standard employment procedures will make your presence here seem less suspicious. As for you, Nancy, Mr. Fitzhugh has asked that I personally give you a tour of the store. The security force is headed by Joe Dane. I've already told him that a new staff member has been hired.

"Ah, here we are," said Mr. Lloyd, stopping in front of a glass door marked "Personnel."

"I'll wait outside so that no one will know we're together," Nancy said.

With far more confidence than the girls had seen from him before, Mr. Lloyd pushed the door open and greeted the receptionist. "Good morning, Joan. I've got a couple of new employees for you."

While George and Bess stayed behind to fill out forms and learn store policies, Bennett Lloyd began Nancy's tour of the whole store.

"We'll start with the ground floor and work our way up," Mr. Lloyd said. "I think you'll be impressed with our setup."

"Oh, I am impressed with the store, Mr. Lloyd," Nancy assured him.

Mr. Lloyd smiled at her enthusiasm. "I'm glad you like the store, Nancy, but I was referring to the unseen side of Danner and Bishop. Behind the walls of the selling floor, we have a whole maze of stockrooms and state-of-the-art security devices."

14

Mr. Lloyd led Nancy through the back rooms, pointing out the various rows of neatly stacked stock. He was especially proud of the store's security system. It was a series of sensor devices that could tell if a shoplifter was walking off with any merchandise.

Along the way Mr. Lloyd introduced Nancy to each of the employees they encountered. Nancy kept a careful eye out for anyone who seemed bitter or unhappy with Danner and Bishop. She felt that someone with a grudge might be responsible for the pranks. But everyone Nancy met seemed friendly and pleasant. Nobody stood out as a likely suspect.

The tour took Nancy to the top floor, where the furs and jewels—the most expensive items in the store—were securely displayed.

Wait until Bess sees *this* department, Nancy thought as she looked at the gleaming jewelry and soft, shining fur coats and jackets. Like all the other merchandise in the store, the items on this floor were of top quality.

"This store is really incredible," Nancy said to Bennett Lloyd.

Mr. Lloyd looked pleased. "Did you know that Mr. Fitzhugh originally planned a much different type of store?"

"Really? What did he have in mind?"

"He had wanted a smaller, more exclusive

store." Bennett Lloyd looked down at his well-polished shoes. "Actually, it was my idea to expand Danner and Bishop and make it into Chicago's top department store. The combination of quality and quantity is the key to our success."

Nancy noticed that the store manager was blushing shyly as he made his admission. "I'll bet most people don't know that," she said gently.

"No, I suppose not many do," Mr. Lloyd acknowledged.

"Well, your idea sure worked," Nancy said.

"Yes, the store has been very prosperous," Mr. Lloyd said with pride.

"Thanks to you," Nancy said with a smile. Then, on impulse, she asked, "Mr. Lloyd, do you have any idea who might be responsible for the pranks?"

Mr. Lloyd met Nancy's steady gaze. "To tell you the truth, I think it's some kids from the private school down the street. We caught them shoplifting a few months ago. We reported the incident to the police and turned them over to their parents."

"And you think the pranks might be their way of getting even?" Nancy guessed.

"I think it's very possible. Those kids are enterprising enough to cut a chandelier chain. But I wouldn't want to accuse them without proof." Mr. Lloyd cleared his throat and changed the subject. "Bess should be settling into the shoe department by now. I'd like you to meet the department supervisor there."

The shoe department was on the third floor. It was bordered on two sides by several massive mahogany display cases, which leaned against pillars.

Nancy saw that Bess was already working, which didn't surprise her. Bess was a good worker. She had had part-time jobs at several stores in River Heights. And Ann Fitzhugh had said the shoe department desperately needed a salesperson.

"You'll absolutely love these suede heels," Bess was saying to a customer. "Look at the sequins! They add just enough glitter to make these shoes a standout. They're irresistible."

Nancy smiled at her friend's hard-sell technique. Nancy was sure that Bess would make the sale.

Just then, Bennett Lloyd said, "Nancy, I'd like you to meet Lindy Dixon, the head of our shoe department. Lindy, this is Nancy Drew, a new member of our security staff." As Lloyd was making the introduction, Nancy took a good look at Bess's new boss. Lindy Dixon was an attractive young woman with bright red hair and a slim figure. And it appeared she liked to wear a lot of makeup.

"Welcome to the team, Nancy," Lindy said in a husky voice.

17

"Thanks," Nancy said, "I'm really looking forward to working here. How long have you been with Danner and Bishop?"

"Long enough," Lindy responded dryly.

"Oh? Don't you like it here?"

"It's okay for now. But I'm not planning to stay forever. I'm an actress," Lindy said.

"Oh, really?" Nancy asked. Lindy was the first employee she had met who didn't seem to be happy with her job at Danner and Bishop.

"I guess I shouldn't be saying all of this in front of Mr. Lloyd, should I?" Lindy smiled brightly at the store manager. "But I'm only working here to save money. Once I've saved enough, I'm heading to New York City. Then, look out, Broadway!"

Nancy laughed at Lindy's enthusiasm, and even Mr. Lloyd smiled.

"How do you think our new salesperson will work out, Lindy?" Bennett Lloyd asked.

"Pretty well, I guess," Lindy said, looking over at where Bess was wrapping up her sale. "I've been trying to get rid of those sequined horrors for two weeks!"

Nancy barely managed to stifle a giggle. She glanced at Mr. Lloyd and saw him fighting back a laugh, too.

They watched as Bess proudly handed her customer the shoes carefully packed in a green and gold Danner and Bishop bag. "I'm sure you're going to enjoy these, ma'am. Thank you for shopping with us."

Nancy watched as Bess turned toward her boss, grinned, and flashed a thumbs-up victory sign. Then Bess's expression suddenly turned to one of horror. "Watch out!" she screamed, pointing.

Nancy turned to see one of the huge mahogany display cases toppling toward her!

3

Speeding Stairs

Nancy felt herself being shoved from behind onto the floor. A split second later, the display case crashed to the floor with a thunderous noise.

Nancy lay on the floor for a moment, dazed. Lindy was lying next to her. Bess stood beside them, pale and panting.

"Are you okay?" Bess asked.

"I think so," Nancy replied. "Lindy, are you all right?"

"Oh, sure." Lindy was sitting up and brushing herself off. "We're lucky Mr. Lloyd was there to push us out of the way. Wait a second—where is he?"

Nancy got to her feet. She saw Bennett Lloyd

lying motionless on the floor, partially covered by the broken wood and glass of the smashed display case.

Nancy rushed over to him and began to pull the store manager out from under the debris. "Mr. Lloyd, are you all right?"

Bennett Lloyd began to move slowly. He moaned quietly and then said, "I . . . I think so. Just a bit shaken, I guess."

Nancy helped the older man sit up. She saw him wince when she touched his shoulder. "We'd better call a doctor for you. You've been hurt."

"No, no," Mr. Lloyd protested. "I'm quite all right. Just give me a moment to catch my breath. I'm fine, really."

"But your shoulder was hit," Lindy said.

"It's just a bruise," Bennett Lloyd said firmly.

By this time a large crowd was gathering in the shoe department, eager to see what was happening. Nancy heard a woman say, "This store is dangerous! Come on, Sandra, let's finish our shopping at Paley's!"

Nancy knew she should investigate the accident quickly before any of the evidence was moved. She decided to take advantage of the commotion around her to quietly inspect the fallen display case.

The valuable mahogany wood had splintered

21

into pieces, and the glass shelves had shattered into bits. Certain that the heavy case could not have fallen by itself, Nancy made a thorough search of the wreckage.

She noticed immediately that the back legs were still attached to the display case. But the front legs had been cut through cleanly. Nancy wondered how long the giant cabinet had been balanced on two disconnected supports. It obviously would have been easy to push over.

Nancy carefully checked the pillar behind where the display case had stood. She knew from her tour that there were four pillars like this one on each floor of the store. They were hollow, and each one contained a sophisticated sensor device.

There was a back panel in the pillar. Nancy quietly slid open the panel and slipped into the pillar.

It wasn't long before she noticed the hole in the side opposite where the display case had stood—a hole large enough for a hand to fit through.

One strong push was all that had been needed to push the display case over. Now Nancy was sure that the falling display case had not been an accident. And that this "prankster" was becoming dangerous.

Nancy carefully searched every inch of the wall. Then she let herself out of the pillar and went back to the display case. In the tangled mess of wood, glass, and shoes, she finally found what she was looking for—a joker card stuck to a piece of wood from the back of the case.

Nancy's mouth set in a tight, grim line.

Meanwhile, Bess had been caught up in the commotion of customers and employees gathered at the accident site. Now she sidled up to Nancy.

"And I thought nothing scary could ever happen in a store like Danner and Bishop," Bess whispered. "All of a sudden, this doesn't seem like so much fun anymore, Nancy."

"I know how you feel," Nancy whispered back, glancing around cautiously. "But hang in there, Bess. We've got to catch this guy."

Just then, the girls saw Ann Fitzhugh striding across the selling floor toward the shoe department. "Oh no!" she cried. "What in the world happened?"

Lindy told Ann the whole story. When Lindy had finished, Ann turned to the store manager.

"Are you feeling all right, Mr. Lloyd?" she asked in a concerned tone. "Maybe you should take the rest of the day off."

"I'm fine now," Bennett Lloyd said with a smile. "Besides, there's too much to do. I really can't take any time off."

"Well, if you're sure . . ."

"I'm sure," Mr. Lloyd said.

"Then, if no one is hurt, I think we should all get back to work," Ann said, taking control of the situation. "Lindy, please call maintenance and have them clean up this mess. I'll get the art department to design a new display for the shoes." She turned to Nancy. "Ms. Drew, since you were an eyewitness, I'd like you to come to my office to file a complete report of the accident."

"Certainly, Ms. Fitzhugh," Nancy replied.

"Let's go, then," Ann said.

When they got to Ann's office, Nancy told the young woman everything she had discovered about the rigging of the accident. "And there was a joker card there, too. The same card that was left after all the other pranks," she finished.

"Oh, Nancy, I'm really getting worried," Ann said. "Someone could have been seriously injured—or even killed—this afternoon. We've got to find this saboteur quickly."

"We don't have much to go on right now," Nancy admitted. "Although Bess and I were right there when the case fell, we didn't see anyone enter or leave the security pillar. These jester cards are the most important clue I have right now. I want to try to find out where they come from. May I use your phone?"

"Of course," Ann said. "I'd better go back downstairs and try to reassure everyone that this was just a freak accident. I don't want the em-

24

ployees getting scared off as well as the customers!"

After Ann had left, Nancy looked through the Chicago yellow pages for novelty shops. She found twelve listed in the downtown area. Fifteen minutes later, Nancy left Danner and Bishop and headed for the first novelty shop on her list.

At Klein's Novelties and Tricks, Nancy showed one of the jester cards to Mr. Klein, the store owner. "Can you tell me if this card was purchased here?" Nancy asked.

The elderly store owner studied the card closely. "Most unusual," he said finally. "I've never seen a card like this. I sell a variety of playing cards here, but nothing like this."

"Where do you think a card like this might come from?" Nancy asked.

"I have no idea," the man replied. "But I don't think it could have come from any of the shops around here."

"Well, thanks for your time," Nancy said. She left the shop and started heading toward the next store on her list.

She soon found out that Mr. Klein had been right. Nobody recognized the card, and nobody had any idea where it had come from. There was only one shop left to visit.

With a sigh, Nancy pushed open the door to the tenth shop on her list and showed the joker card to the girl behind the counter.

"I think," the girl said slowly, inspecting the card carefully, "I think that this might be a custom-printed card."

"You mean, it would have to be ordered specially? It couldn't just be bought at a retail store?" Nancy asked. She realized this would mean that the practical joker had planned everything more carefully than she had thought.

"I'll tell you who does this sort of work." The girl pulled out a phone book and opened it on the counter. "Yeah, here it is. Pozanski Graphics—it's over on Twelfth Street, not too far from here."

"Thanks a lot!" Nancy said as she rushed out of the shop.

A few minutes later, Nancy was standing in the small office of Pozanski Graphics, explaining her problem to one of the designers.

"I don't know if I can help you," the dark-haired woman said. "I'll be happy to take a look at the card," she added, taking it from Nancy, "but we print so many different things here, I just don't know if I'll recognize one particular card."

The woman perched her glasses on her nose and peered at the card.

"You know, I do remember this one," she said, nodding.

Nancy felt flooded with relief. "Are you sure?" she asked cautiously.

"Oh, yes. I remember them very well. Strange looking, aren't they? I remember wondering what

26

in the world anyone would want such a large quantity of these nightmare faces for."

"I've been wondering that, too," Nancy said. "Could you tell me how many of these cards were made?"

"Well, let me see. I should have the purchase order here in my files." The woman hunted through some papers for a moment and then announced, "Here it is." She pulled a folder out of the pile and opened it. "Two dozen of those jester cards were ordered by mail."

"By mail!" Nancy exclaimed. "Can you tell me who ordered them?"

"I'm afraid it doesn't say," the woman said, scanning the paper. "There was no name on the order, and the cards were paid for by money order. I don't know what else I can tell you. I'm sorry." The woman shrugged.

"But . . ." Nancy was puzzled for a moment. "Can you tell me where the cards were mailed to?"

"I wish I could help you, Ms. Drew," the woman said sincerely, "but it's strict company policy never to reveal any customer information. I'm sure you understand that we have to protect our customers' privacy."

"I understand," Nancy said. She was so close to an answer—she just couldn't let this opportunity slip through her fingers. "Well, thank you for your help."

Nancy reached out to shake the woman's hand and "accidentally" stumbled forward off balance. "Oh no!" she exclaimed as she knocked the folder out of the woman's hand. The papers scattered on the floor.

"Oh, I'm so sorry," Nancy said, crouching down to gather up the papers.

"No, no, that's all right, dear," the woman said, bending down. "I've got them."

"Let me help," Nancy insisted, hastily shuffling through the papers.

Finally the papers were all gathered and neatly back in the folder. Nancy thanked the woman again and walked out of the office, lost in thought.

All the way back to Danner and Bishop, Nancy thought about the startling new information she had just gathered in the graphics shop. She wouldn't have believed it if she hadn't seen it in writing on the purchase order.

The cards had been delivered to Danner and Bishop!

Back at the store, Nancy was eager to tell the Fitzhughs what she had discovered—that someone inside the store had to be involved in the pranks.

Nancy stepped onto the escalator leading up to the second floor. As she was being lifted above the ground, Nancy glanced around the first floor. There were fewer shoppers browsing around than there had been earlier. The latest prank had definitely scared more people away.

Suddenly, Nancy became aware that the escalator was picking up speed. Looking behind her, she saw that she was alone on the escalator. Nancy grasped the handrails tightly.

The escalator was going faster and faster. Nancy felt herself whizzing past mirrors and hanging plants, all going by in a blur. Ahead of her she saw an enormous marble pillar just beyond the escalator's landing.

Nancy knew she was in danger. She tried to brace herself as the step she was on neared the top.

She realized that she would have to jump clear of the escalator at just the right moment in order to avoid being hurt.

Suddenly, the escalator jerked to a stop, catching Nancy off guard and hurling her toward the marble pillar!

4

Some Really Hot Shoes

Nancy lowered her head and tucked her body into a ball. She landed hard and tumbled across the tile floor, just managing to sideswipe the marble pillar. But as she came out of her somersault, she crashed into a display of mannequins, knocking them to the floor.

A saleswoman hurried over to her. "Are you hurt?" she asked anxiously.

"I think I'm all right," Nancy said, sitting up and rubbing her elbows. "The room is spinning around a little, but that will go away in a minute." She looked at the fallen display of mannequins. There were arms and legs strewn all around her. It looked as if a tornado had swept through the dress department of Danner and Bishop.

"I'll call maintenance," the saleswoman said. "And that escalator will have to be repaired right away."

Nancy stood up slowly, still feeling a little dazed. "I'll make sure nobody else gets on the escalator until it's fixed," she told the saleswoman.

Nancy walked back to the top of the escalator and blinked in disbelief. The steps were moving at normal speed.

Nancy stared at the escalator for a long time, wondering what was going on. She wasn't sure if the speeding escalator had simply been broken, or if this was the work of the store's saboteur. Nancy shook her head. The pattern was all wrong. There had never been two pranks on the same day before. It was beginning to look like today's pranks were aimed directly at her!

Could someone be trying to stop her? Nancy wondered. But no one in the store was supposed to know that Nancy was a detective—no one except the Fitzhughs and Bennett Lloyd, and none of them seemed capable of rigging a runaway escalator.

Nancy had started to search the area for a jester card when two men arrived. One was wearing a maintenance uniform; the other was obviously a member of the security staff. The maintenance worker smiled at Nancy and asked,

"Are you the young lady who was hurt on the escalator?"

"Yes," Nancy said, "but I think the mannequins were hurt worse than I was. Just a few bumps and bruises for me."

"I'm glad to hear that," the maintenance worker said. He had blond hair and blue eyes, and Nancy guessed that he was about thirty years old.

"I'm Nick Holt," he added. "Danner and Bishop maintenance chief. And this is Joe Dane, head of security."

Joe Dane nodded at Nancy. He was a tall, heavyset man who looked to be in his mid-fifties. He had a short crewcut and small eyes set in a beefy face.

"I'm pleased to meet you both," Nancy said. "I'm Nancy Drew, and I'm just starting work here at the store."

"Oh yeah?" Nick Holt asked. "Where will you be working?"

"Security," Nancy answered. "I was on my way up to the personnel office to report for work."

Joe Dane looked at Nancy closely. There was a sour expression on his face. "I never heard anything about a new person in security," he muttered. "They never tell me anything around here. You'd think I had no control over my own department. Who hired you, anyway?"

"Calm down, Joe," Nick Holt said, giving Joe

Dane a playful punch on the arm. "The lady's brand-new on the job. Give her a break."

Nancy looked up at Joe Dane. She knew she had to protect her undercover role and that she would have to be particularly careful around her new boss.

"Mr. Lloyd hired me," Nancy said.

Joe Dane's face started to turn red with anger. "Lloyd should have consulted me first," he sputtered. "With new recruits like this, it's no wonder the store is falling apart."

Before Nancy could say anything, Joe Dane turned his back on her and approached the escalator. He opened a panel and began punching some buttons and muttering to himself.

Nick Holt chuckled. "I don't know what Joe thinks he's doing, but he'll never be able to fix the escalator that way."

Nancy couldn't tell him that she was sure the escalator had been rigged for only her ride. It wasn't really broken.

Seeing Nancy's frown, Nick Holt said quickly, "Don't worry about old Joe. His bark is worse than his bite."

"What's wrong with him?" Nancy couldn't help asking.

"As head of security, he's starting to look bad with all of these crazy tricks going on. In fact, his job is on the line. He could be fired."

Nancy nodded thoughtfully. Then she watched as Joe Dane continued to fiddle with the escalator switches. He was getting more and more frustrated by the lack of results. He obviously didn't know what he was doing.

"I'm curious about the security here, since I'll be working in that department. Does the store have a good security system?" Nancy asked Nick.

Nick Holt nodded. "Yes, the staff here is one of the best in the business. Joe runs a tight ship. There are sensor devices on every door to catch shoplifters. There's also an elaborate alarm system throughout the store, so if anybody breaks in after hours the Chicago police are alerted right away. And then there are the Dobermans."

"Dobermans!" Nancy said in a shocked tone.

"You bet. We have three specially trained attack dogs. They roam the store at night."

The thought of vicious Dobermans let loose in the store gave Nancy the creeps. Nick noticed her reaction and grinned at her.

"The dogs freak everyone out at first," he said. "But they're more effective than human guards because they're quick to arrive at the scene of a crime and can detect hiding burglars by using their sense of smell. Once caught, nobody can get away from them."

"I'm sure," Nancy said, glad that Bess hadn't been around to hear about this.

"I'd better get to work cleaning up this mess you made," Nick said teasingly as he headed back to the fallen mannequins.

Nancy turned and looked at Joe Dane again in time to see him close the panel in disgust. He shoved his hand into his pocket and pulled out a large white handkerchief. As he did, Nancy saw a matchbook and some paper fall out of his pocket onto the floor.

Joe walked off without looking back, and Nancy headed for the spot where he had been standing. She bent over and picked up the items. There was a paper cigar ring, an empty matchbook, and a gum wrapper. And Nancy found something else lying near the control panel—a jester card.

"That looks pretty nasty," said a voice behind Nancy. It was Nick Holt, peering over her shoulder. Nancy was beginning to feel that this maintenance worker was taking *too* much interest in her activities.

"Yes, it does," Nancy agreed. She wondered if the card had fallen out of Joe Dane's pocket. If he were the prankster, he could have dropped it on purpose. Or he could have placed it on the floor while he was trying to fix the escalator. But Nancy hadn't been able to search the area around the escalator until after Joe Dane had been there, so she couldn't be sure when the card had appeared. And Nick Holt also had had an opportunity to plant the jester.

Nancy looked at the matchbook in her hand, hoping that it might be a clue. It said "Omni Aviation" on the front. On the inside cover was a phone number.

"Here, let me throw that away for you," Nick Holt said. He reached for the matchbook, the cigar ring, and the gum wrapper, but Nancy pulled her hand back.

"That's okay, I'll do it," she said casually but firmly. She wanted to hold on to anything that might be a clue or used as evidence.

Nick Holt shrugged. "Okay. Well, I'd better get back to this mess, or my own job will be on the line." He chuckled and then became serious, adding, "But I hope these stupid tricks stop soon before every display in the store is broken!"

That night Nancy, Bess, and George had dinner with Carlin and Ann Fitzhugh in the elegant dining room of the Fitzhugh mansion. Before dinner, the girls had been shown up to their rooms. The rooms were so beautifully decorated that Nancy had to agree with Bess that they were fabulous.

There were freshly cut flowers on the long polished table in the dining room. Two servants hovered quietly nearby. The whole room was lit by the soft light of candles. Nancy was grateful for the relaxing atmosphere after her harrowing day.

Nancy filled everyone in on the day's events. She told them about her card hunt, the runaway escalator, and her conversation with Nick Holt and Joe Dane. The Fitzhughs seemed to be impressed by the amount of information that Nancy had been able to gather, but Nancy was quick to point out that the investigation had only just begun.

"We only have a few pieces of the puzzle so far, Mr. Fitzhugh," Nancy said, picking up her water glass.

"But you found out something really important, Nancy," Ann Fitzhugh said. "This joker has to be someone inside the store."

"Or someone wants it to seem that way," Nancy said. She took a sip of water. Then she went on, "I think it's a good place to start, though. I want to get to know a little bit about every employee. You know, try to find out who isn't happy at Danner and Bishop or who might be holding a grudge. That's where George and Bess go to work."

"You mean all we have to do is get to know people?" Bess asked, looking up from her steak. "I can handle that."

"I'll be able to get to a lot of people, Nan,"

George assured her. "You'd be surprised how much people will say to the cleaning person."

"Do you have anyone special in mind, Nancy?" Carlin Fitzhugh asked.

"Well . . ." Nancy hesitated. She didn't want to make accusations without evidence, but she felt her clients had a right to know what she was thinking. "I do have a few suspects."

"Already?" Ann Fitzhugh asked in surprise, her fork halfway to her mouth.

"I don't have any concrete evidence yet, but I do have a few ideas," Nancy said.

"Let's hear them," Carlin Fitzhugh said, leaning toward her.

"Well, Joe Dane is one of my suspects," Nancy said.

"Joe Dane? That big guy who's head of security?" George looked surprised. "He was a little rude when I met him, but he didn't seem to be the type to pull pranks."

"I *think* he may have dropped the jester card near the escalator. Also, he has access to every hidden area of the store. He's in a perfect position to make trouble."

Mr. Fitzhugh looked like he wanted to object, but at the last moment he refrained from commenting on Nancy's first suspect.

"Who else do you have on your Most Wanted List, Nancy?" Ann asked.

Nancy cleared her throat before answering. "Well, Nick Holt and Bennett Lloyd are also possibilities."

"Nick Holt? Bennett Lloyd?" Ann Fitzhugh asked in a surprised tone.

"I know it's hard to imagine Mr. Lloyd as a practical joker," Nancy began.

"Impossible to imagine is more like it," Carlin Fitzhugh interrupted. "Really, Nancy, Bennett Lloyd wouldn't have the nerve to carry out all these practical jokes. Besides, he's dedicated to the store—I can't imagine him doing anything to harm our business."

"I agree with you," Nancy admitted. "But it looks like today's pranks were aimed at stopping *me*. He's the only person besides us who knows why I'm here," she explained.

"But, Nancy, he was the one who saved you and Lindy from the falling display case," Bess argued. "He even got hurt himself."

"That's true," Nancy agreed. "But I'm keeping Bennett Lloyd on my list of suspects just to be safe," she stated firmly.

"Why is Nick Holt a suspect?" Ann Fitzhugh demanded.

"Just a hunch." Nancy shrugged before adding, "And I think he knows enough about escalators to rig an accident."

"I think that we've all had enough of this

problem for one day," Carlin Fitzhugh said. "I suggest we get our minds off this case by moving on to dessert. Anybody for chocolate cake?"

Nancy and George burst out laughing as Bess quickly shouted, "Yes!"

The next morning Nancy started work as a security guard. She was peeking into the shoe department stockroom on her rounds when George came up to her. She raised her eyebrows when she saw the gray uniform Nancy was wearing.

"It's a good thing Bess doesn't have to work in security," Nancy said. "She'd never be willing to wear this horrible uniform."

"You can say that again," Bess muttered as she came out of the stockroom, six shoe boxes piled high in her arms. "Don't you two ever work? Do you really have time to stand around chatting like this?" she grumbled.

"I *am* working," George said cheerfully. "I was ordered to empty the wastepaper baskets on this floor. I'm just wandering around trying to find them."

"How's it going, Bess?" Nancy asked, looking out at the quiet shoe department. There were only three customers in the area, and everything seemed peaceful.

"It's not as much fun being in the store as I thought it would be," Bess complained. "I love to shop, but working in the shoe department is hard. I have to do everything."

"Where's Lindy?" Nancy asked.

"She's never around much," Bess replied with a shrug. "She's auditioning for a play, and she hangs out in the stockroom practicing her lines. When Lindy does bother to come out, she doesn't do any work. She just stands around telling anyone who will listen about how she's going to go to New York and become a big star. Meanwhile, I have to do all of the work."

"Well, look at the bright side, Bess," George said. "At least you don't have to wear an ugly uniform like Nancy's."

"That's the only good part of the job," Bess said. "I'd better get these shoes to those ladies."

Nancy watched her friend walk out onto the selling floor.

"I guess I should start working, too," George said. "I'll see you later."

As the girls stepped away from the stockroom door, two identically dressed twelve-year-old boys streaked past them and raced toward the elevator.

"Hey!" Nancy yelled as she took off after the fleeing children.

Suddenly, a piercing scream sounded from behind the shoe department's display cases. "Get them off! Get them off me!" one of Bess's customers was shrieking.

Nancy gave up her chase and turned back toward Bess. "What's happening?" she called out.

"I don't know," Bess cried. She was watching in horror as her three customers hopped around, grabbing at their shoes as if their feet were on fire.

5

Jack Paley

The women screamed and jumped up and down. Finally, one of them managed to kick off her shoes. She collapsed into the nearest chair, breathing heavily.

Bess and George tried to calm the other two women, but it was impossible to get either of them to explain what was happening.

Nancy picked up one of the shoes the customer had kicked off and inspected it. Immediately she spotted a flaky white substance coating the inside. She touched the inside of the shoe carefully and felt a burning, itching sensation on the tip of her finger.

"Itching powder," Nancy stated. "Someone has put itching powder in these new shoes!"

Bess and Nancy pulled the shoes off the feet of the other two women, who were finally sitting still. "But I just brought these shoes out of the stockroom. Nobody could have tampered with them out here."

"My guess is that a lot of the shoes in the stockroom are full of itching powder," Nancy said grimly.

"Nancy, those boys!" George said suddenly. "The ones who were running away. They could have done it!"

"Let's go!" Nancy said. "Bess, you stay here and help these ladies," Nancy called over her shoulder as she and George started running toward the escalator.

The girls scrambled down to the first floor in record time and dashed toward the front door.

"Did you see two boys come running by here?" Nancy asked a security guard by the door.

"They were both dressed in white shirts, blue pants, and blue ties," George added.

"I saw them," the guard answered. "They left the store about a minute ago."

"Thanks," Nancy called as she pushed through the revolving door. George followed closely behind her.

The girls barreled down the front steps to the sidewalk.

"Look!" cried George.

Nancy turned to see where her friend was

pointing. About a block and a half away, two figures in white shirts and blue pants were climbing the steps of a building. Before the boys had disappeared through the door, Nancy and George took off after them.

They pounded down the sidewalk as fast as they could toward the building.

A sign over the door said "The Peale-Benson School." Nancy realized that the boys' matching clothes were the school's uniform.

Nancy and George rushed through the door and stopped to catch their breath. Before them was a long hall with a number of doors. Their eyes scanned the empty hallway searching for any possible clue to the boys' whereabouts.

"There," Nancy said, pointing. "See that door at the end? It's still swinging."

"They must have gone that way," George replied.

The girls moved quickly to the end of the hall and found themselves at the head of a staircase, leading down into darkness.

Nancy paused, then glanced at George and said, "They've got to be down there."

George nodded. "Let's go."

Nancy took a deep breath. Then she reached into the dark for a banister and stepped forward.

"Stop right there!" a deep voice said suddenly. "Stop, or I'll call the police."

45

Nancy and George turned quickly to see a tall older man in a gray suit glowering down at them.

"We work for Danner and Bishop," Nancy said in her most businesslike voice. She was glad she was wearing the security uniform with the store logo identifying her. "We have reason to believe that a couple of boys who have been destroying Danner and Bishop property are hiding here."

After Nancy had explained why she and George were chasing the boys, the man nodded his head thoughtfully.

"That does sound suspicious," he sadly agreed. "I'm David Marks, the headmaster of the school. If some of my boys are causing trouble with local businesses, I want to get to the bottom of it. Let's see if they are in the basement as you seem to think."

Mr. Marks led the girls down the stairs, turning on the lights as he went. The basement was shadowy and dim, and there was no sign of the boys Nancy and George had been chasing.

"No one here," the headmaster said after they had checked the entire room.

"Just a minute," Nancy said. "There's one place we haven't looked." She walked over to a narrow wooden door that was almost hidden behind a stand of mops and brooms. She yanked the door open. There, crouching low in the far corner of the tiny closet, were the missing boys.

"We didn't do anything," one of the boys protested before Nancy had a chance to say anything. He had curly red hair and a freckled face.

"Get out of there, you two," the headmaster ordered sternly. "We'll find out just what you did or didn't do."

Mr. Marks brought the boys out into the dimly lit basement. "Are these the two you saw in the store?" he asked.

"They're the ones," George said angrily.

"We didn't do anything," the red-haired boy repeated.

"Well, Ian, if you didn't do anything we'll know that soon enough," the headmaster said calmly. "But these ladies seem to think you've been causing trouble at Danner and Bishop."

"We haven't," Ian insisted.

"Then why were you running away from us?" Nancy asked.

"We weren't running away from you. We were running because we were late getting back to school." He turned to his friend. "Right, Tom?"

Tom didn't say anything. He just shrugged and nodded. He was a thin, blond boy with a pale face.

"If you were late for school, why were you hiding in the basement?" demanded George. Ian and Tom looked at the floor in silence.

"Mr. Marks," Nancy said, "have Ian and Tom ever been in trouble with Danner and Bishop before?"

"I don't know for sure, but I wouldn't be surprised," the headmaster said. "Ian McDonough and Tom Paley are known around here as troublemakers."

"If it's all right with you, I'd like to bring Ian and Tom back to the store to see the general manager." Nancy remembered Bennett Lloyd's comment about private school boys being caught shoplifting. She wondered if these could be the same boys. "I think we'll be able to get to the bottom of this with his help."

"I'll go with you," Mr. Marks said. "I'd like to get to the bottom of this myself!" Then he turned to the two boys and announced, "I'm hoping for your sakes that today's activities were limited to cutting class. If not, you'll learn what trouble really means!"

The five of them walked back to Danner and Bishop, Ian McDonough insisting on his and Tom's innocence the whole way.

Back at the store, they found Bennett Lloyd on the executive floor, just outside Carlin Fitzhugh's office.

"I thought I told you never to set foot in this store again," Bennett Lloyd exclaimed as soon as he spotted the group.

Nancy and George looked at each other in

surprise. They had never heard the store manager sound so angry before. Even Carlin Fitzhugh stepped out of his office to see what the commotion was.

"You punk," Bennett Lloyd continued as he approached Tom Paley. "Shoplifters are thrown out of here." He grabbed Tom by the front of his shirt.

"It was only a little radio," Tom muttered. "You got it back. And I didn't steal anything today."

Nancy put her hand on Bennett Lloyd's arm to try to calm him down. Mr. Lloyd took a deep breath and released Tom.

"Tom," Nancy said, looking the boy directly in the eyes. "Did you put itching powder in the ladies' shoes?"

The boy snickered. "Why would I do a stupid thing like that?" He glared at the group. "You think that just because my father owns Paley's you can treat me this way," he added angrily.

There was a stunned silence. Tom's statement had caught everyone off guard.

Nancy was the first one to speak. "Your father owns Paley's store across town?"

"Yeah," Tom Paley said with a grunt.

"That proves it," Bennett Lloyd said triumphantly. "Danner and Bishop and Paley's are in direct competition. It would make sense for Paley to want to cause trouble over here."

Carlin Fitzhugh stepped forward and spoke for the first time. "It looks as if you've caught our practical joker, Nancy. I can't say I'm surprised that he's the culprit. Jack Paley has tried several times to buy Danner and Bishop. He wants to add it to his chain of Paley's department stores. He's probably hoping to make me want to sell by arranging all of these pranks." He looked at Tom. "And he's been sending his son to carry them out!"

"I took a radio *once*, all right?" Tom Paley said hotly. "But I didn't have anything to do with those dumb jokes!"

"Well, why don't we just call your father and see about that," Carlin Fitzhugh said.

"I'll make the call," Nancy volunteered. "I'll ask him to come over here."

"Use the phone in my office," Mr. Fitzhugh suggested. "Grace will give you Paley's office number."

Nancy got the phone number from the secretary. Then she took advantage of the quiet emptiness of Mr. Fitzhugh's office to pull her thoughts together.

She realized that the boys couldn't possibly have pulled off all the practical jokes. They never would have been able to rig the escalator. They didn't have the technical know-how to do it. In any case, they couldn't have gotten access to the controls.

Then there were the jester cards. They had been delivered to Danner and Bishop. How could the boys have gotten their hands on the cards?

But Tom's father, Jack Paley, *could* have masterminded the pranks and used an accomplice in the store to carry them out.

Nancy dialed Paley's number. When she reached the store owner, she told him about his son's possible involvement in the problem at Danner and Bishop.

"What? He's in trouble *again?*" Paley exclaimed so loudly Nancy had to jerk the phone away from her ear. "I'll be right over to get him!" Nancy heard him slam down the receiver. She hung up and shook her head. She couldn't help feeling sorry for Tom. His father had sounded really angry.

Jack Paley arrived at Danner and Bishop a half an hour later. He was a short, dark-haired man, and he was wearing a dark gray business suit. Paley was still as outraged as he had been on the phone.

"What's all this about?" he demanded in a loud, angry voice. Then he turned to Headmaster Marks and roared, "What's the matter with the teachers at Peale-Benson? He should be at school, not in this two-bit store!"

"Please calm down, Mr. Paley," Nancy said. "I'm sure we can discuss this without—"

"Don't tell me to calm down!" Paley exploded.

He glared at his son. "What have you done this time?"

"I didn't do anything, Dad, honest," Tom Paley said. Nancy couldn't help noticing how frightened Tom seemed to be of his father—and she couldn't blame him.

"I've had it with you!" Paley bellowed at Tom. "Why can't you stay out of trouble?" Abruptly, Paley turned to Carlin Fitzhugh. "What's going on here, Fitzhugh? Can't you run your store without getting me involved in your problems?"

"Well, frankly, Jack, we do have some problems, and I'm not too sure you're not involved," Carlin Fitzhugh said.

"What do you mean?" Mr. Paley demanded suspiciously.

"I'm sure you've heard about the string of mishaps we've been having here lately," Mr. Fitzhugh said.

"I've heard rumors," Jack Paley replied. "What does that have to do with me?"

"Your son is a suspect in the latest prank," Nancy explained. "It seems pretty unlikely that he would want to damage Danner and Bishop. But *you* might want to see the store suffer."

Paley stared at Nancy furiously. "Are you accusing me of dirty tactics?"

"No one is saying that, Mr. Paley," Nancy replied quickly. "We just want to get to the bottom of this."

"I run a clean business," Paley stated angrily, "and I won't be treated this way. I will not stand for accusations from some interfering teenager!"

"Jack, calm down, will you?" Mr. Fitzhugh said. "We only——"

"I will not calm down!" roared Paley. He turned toward Nancy. "And I'll teach *you* to make false accusations against me!"

His face bright red with rage, Jack Paley lunged at Nancy!

6

Deadly Games

"Dad, don't!" Nancy heard Tom Paley cry out as she stepped away from his father.

Nancy took a deep breath. "I don't think you really want to attack me, Mr. Paley," she said quietly, looking the angry man in the eyes.

Jack Paley stopped suddenly and turned toward Carlin Fitzhugh. Nancy could have sworn she heard the entire group sigh with relief.

"You'd better learn to keep your employees in line," Jack Paley said loudly. "She was clearly provoking me into a fight!" His voice didn't boom with the confidence Nancy had heard earlier.

"That's not the way it looked to us," Carlin Fitzhugh commented.

Paley whirled around to face him. "You'll be

hearing from my lawyer about the charges you've been making against me," Mr. Paley sputtered. "I'm going to sue you for slander!"

"You can try," Fitzhugh said evenly. "But I doubt if you'll succeed. In the meantime, the next time your son sets foot in my store, he's going straight to jail."

Paley narrowed his eyes. "We'll see about that," he said threateningly. "Come on, Tom. We're getting out of here."

Jack Paley turned without even looking at his son and stormed off toward the elevator. Tom followed his father, his head bowed.

"If there's nothing more you need us for, I think Ian and I should be leaving as well," David Marks said.

"Thank you for bringing the boys back here and helping us out," Nancy said to him.

After the headmaster had led Ian away, Nancy turned to the store owner. "I'm sorry we weren't able to learn more about how Paley is connected."

Carlin Fitzhugh smiled sympathetically. "Well, not from lack of trying."

"You can say that again," George said. "Nothing like cornering a couple of suspects in a broom closet."

Mr. Fitzhugh laughed. "You girls are certainly putting a lot of effort into this case, and I do appreciate that." He glanced at his watch. "All this nonsense with Paley has held me up. I'm late for a meeting. I've got to run."

As Mr. Fitzhugh disappeared down the hall, Bennett Lloyd spoke up. "You ladies have had a difficult morning. You could probably use a nice relaxing lunch. Why don't you let me treat you in the cafeteria? Bring your friend Bess along, too. She had quite a time settling down those women with the itchy feet."

"Thanks, Mr. Lloyd," Nancy said. "But would it be a good idea for all four of us to be seen together?"

"Don't worry about that," Mr. Lloyd said, smiling. "I regularly take new store employees—especially the hard-working ones—out to lunch. No one will think anything of it."

Nancy and George agreed and headed down to the shoe department to find Bess. She was happy to see her friends.

"You won't believe what's been going on here!" Bess said, grimacing. "Almost all of the shoes in the stockroom were coated with itching powder. I've spent hours taking them out of their boxes for cleaning—and do I itch!"

George and Nancy laughed. "Come on," said George. "It's time for a break. Mr. Lloyd is treating us to lunch in the cafeteria."

"Great," Bess said enthusiastically. "I'm starving. I just have to let Lindy know I'm leaving."

Bess headed to the door of the stockroom.

"Lindy? I've been invited to lunch with some other new employees, so is it okay if I go now?" Nancy and George couldn't hear Lindy's reply, but Bess cheerfully called out "Thanks!" and scurried back to her friends. "Well, what are we waiting for? Let's go!"

As they waited for the employee elevator, Nancy said in a low voice to George, "This is a good opportunity to find out something more about Mr. Lloyd."

George raised her eyebrows. "You still don't think he could be the prankster, do you?" she said.

"I think it's pretty unlikely," Nancy admitted. "He loves Danner and Bishop too much to want to hurt it. But he's still a suspect, just like everyone else."

Bennett Lloyd was waiting for them by the door of the cafeteria. The girls hadn't been in the cafeteria before, and Bess sighed with pleasure as they walked into the huge, bright room.

"Wow!" she exclaimed. "This is the nicest employees' cafeteria I've ever seen."

Bennett Lloyd smiled at her. "It *is* nice, isn't it? Danner and Bishop likes to provide pleasant facilities for their employees. I think you'll find that the food is just as nice as the atmosphere."

The girls started down the buffet-style line to get their food.

"Watch out, Bess," George warned, looking at

the fancy desserts spread out on the shelves. "This place could destroy your diet!"

"It's been a tough morning," Bess said with a grin. "I'll just have to put my diet on hold for now."

Bess reached for a piece of lemon meringue pie. Then she changed her mind and went for a cherry tart instead. But before the tart reached her tray, a chocolate mousse caught her eye. Nancy and George watched their friend in amusement.

"Why don't you try all three?" Nancy suggested teasingly.

"Don't tempt me. All that work in the shoe department made me hungry!" Bess finally settled on a thick sandwich and the mousse and set them on her tray.

Nancy and George made their selections— roast beef and tuna fish sandwiches—and the three girls followed Bennett Lloyd along the far wall of the cafeteria.

"I believe fewer employees will notice us here," said Bennett Lloyd as he motioned to a table in the corner.

"This is a great treat, Mr. Lloyd," Bess said, as she settled down at the table. "Everybody has been so nice to us, especially the Fitzhughs. We're staying at their mansion, and it's just gorgeous."

"Yes," Bennett Lloyd said. "It is beautiful."

"How long have you known Mr. Fitzhugh?" Nancy asked, trying to sound casual.

"I was the first person Mr. Fitzhugh hired after he bought the business," Mr. Lloyd said proudly. "That was back thirty years ago, when Danner and Bishop was just a small clothing store."

"It's hard to believe that Danner and Bishop was ever small," George said.

"Oh, it was," Mr. Lloyd said. "But over the years, Mr. Fitzhugh has put a large percentage of the profits back into the store. That's how he was able to expand the operation." He paused for a moment, then added, "I can't say I've gotten rich working here. But, of course, no salary could really reflect my contribution to the store."

"Do you feel that Mr. Fitzhugh treats you well?" Nancy asked as she put down her sandwich.

"Oh, I'm not complaining," Mr. Lloyd added firmly. "I'm devoted to Danner and Bishop. It's my life." He looked proud. "Actually, I feel lucky to have such a responsible position, given my background."

"What do you mean?" Nancy asked.

"Well, I don't have a fancy college education or a business degree like, say, Ann Fitzhugh."

Just then, they all heard a loud voice say, "Hi, everybody! Mind if I join you?"

The girls and Bennett Lloyd looked up to see Lindy Dixon standing next to their table, smiling at them.

Mr. Lloyd cleared his throat. "Ms. Dixon, may I ask who's watching the shoe department while you're up here?" he asked sternly.

"Oh, I got Sue Pelkowski from handbags to fill in for me," Lindy said cheerfully.

Nancy noticed that Bess rolled her eyes when Lindy sat down. The red-haired young woman made a lot of noise with her jangling bracelets. Bess winced when Lindy plunked her large purple tote bag on the table. Nancy remembered Bess's complaints about Lindy earlier that morning.

Lindy hadn't brought any food with her. And she only seemed interested in speaking to Bennett Lloyd.

"Mr. Lloyd, you look positively handsome today," Lindy said in a gushing way. "That tie matches your gray eyes beautifully!"

Bennett Lloyd blushed a little and looked uncomfortable. He coughed and adjusted his glasses nervously.

Lindy leaned closer to the store manager, bracelets clanking loudly and earrings swinging. "I was wondering if it would be all right if I left a little early today. You don't mind, do you, Mr. Lloyd?" She flashed him a huge smile.

"Again, Ms. Dixon?"

Lindy leaned even closer. "You see, this is a very special occasion," she said in a loud whisper. "There's a really important audition at the Little Theater this afternoon. I think this could be my big break, and I'd like to get there early. . . ."

After a few minutes of her pleading, Mr. Lloyd finally gave in and gave Lindy permission to leave the store before the end of the work day. She thanked him, got up, and headed out of the cafeteria.

Mr. Lloyd shook his head as he watched her leave. "That young woman thinks *every* audition will be her 'big break.' I only hope her acting on stage is as good as her acting when she wants time off from work." He looked at his watch. "I'm afraid I have to go to a meeting now." He smiled at the girls. "Thank you for joining me for lunch."

"Thanks for inviting us, Mr. Lloyd," Nancy said.

"My pleasure," Mr. Lloyd replied.

"Great," Bess muttered to Nancy and George after Mr. Lloyd had left. "This latest audition of Lindy's means I'll have even *more* work to do. That shoe department is starting to drive me crazy. I don't care if I never see another pair of shoes again!"

Nancy laughed. "I'll believe that when I see—"

Suddenly a loud noise sounded above her head.

Bess shrieked and George jumped as one end of an overhead fluorescent light fixture suddenly dislodged from the ceiling and fell down toward their table. The girls ducked quickly as the light crashed on their trays and chairs. Broken glass scattered everywhere.

Then there was silence. Startled employees looked up from their lunches to see what had happened.

A cafeteria worker came over to them. "Are you three all right?" he asked.

"I think we're okay," Nancy said after looking at George and Bess.

"We're fine," George agreed. Bess gulped and nodded.

"Better move away from that glass," advised the man. "I'll get a mop and broom and clean that up before someone gets a nasty cut." He hurried away.

The girls stood up and carefully moved away from the table. "What a mess!" Nancy said, looking around at all the damage.

"Yeah," Bess agreed. She shook her head. "My poor chocolate mousse—all over the floor!" She looked down at what remained of her dessert.

"Come on, Bess," George said impatiently. "Don't be ridiculous. We could have been hurt."

Bess ignored her cousin. Instead, she bent over and carefully picked up something from the gooey mass of food on the floor. "Look at this," Bess said quietly.

Nancy and George peered over their friend's shoulder to see what she had found. Bess was holding a jester card.

Nancy took the card from Bess. She wiped the chocolate mousse off it, and her eyes widened. This card had a rhyme written on the back. Nancy read it through once, and the words sent a chill up and down her spine:

DIRTY TRICKS ARE LOTS OF FUN,
BUT DEADLY GAMES HAVE JUST BEGUN!

7

The Clue on the Matchbook

"What does it say, Nancy?" George asked.

"Tell you later," Nancy whispered, smoothly slipping the card into the pocket of her blazer. The cafeteria worker was coming back to start cleaning up the mess, and a few employees were walking over to take a look at the damage. "We've still got some time before our lunch hour is over. Why don't we go outside for some fresh air?"

The girls got their coats from the employee locker room and went outside. "There's a coffee shop across the street," Nancy said. "We can talk privately there."

When they got to the coffee shop, the girls settled into a booth and ordered hot chocolate. Nancy showed her friends the poem on the card.

"Oh no," Bess gasped.

"This is getting weird, Nan," George said.

"Yeah, I know," Nancy said. "This joker really seems to be serious about hurting someone."

"And it seems like that someone is you," George said in a concerned voice. "I mean, a lot of the more dangerous pranks have happened to you."

"This time it happened to all three of us," Nancy pointed out. She smiled a little. "Don't worry. I'm sure we'll get this guy before he can really hurt anyone."

"I don't know, Nancy," Bess said unhappily. "I think we should just get out of there."

"That's exactly what this guy wants us to do," George stated. "In fact, he wants everybody to get out of there—especially the customers!"

"Right." Nancy paused for a moment, going over the details of the case in her mind. "And that brings me to the suspect I want to question now."

"Who's that?" George asked. She recognized the look in Nancy's eyes. She knew her friend was on to something.

Nancy spoke quietly. "Jack Paley. He's the one who has the most clear-cut motive for wanting to ruin Danner and Bishop."

"You'd better wear boxing gloves if you're planning to go see that hothead," George said dryly.

Nancy grimaced. "I know what you mean. But I've got to talk to him," she added firmly.

Nancy used her half-hour break that afternoon to head across town to see Jack Paley.

A taxi took her to Paley's department store in five minutes. After Nancy stepped inside the store, she quickly scanned the first floor. It didn't take her long to decide that Paley's wasn't as nice a store as Danner and Bishop.

There was no music, no potted plants, and no soft lighting. Paley's was fast-paced and crowded. It had a totally different atmosphere from the store she was trying to protect.

Nancy found her way to the executive offices and approached the woman sitting outside Jack Paley's office door. "I'd like to see Mr. Paley, please."

The woman peered at Nancy over her glasses. "Do you have an appointment, Ms. . . . ?"

"Drew," Nancy said.

"I'm sorry, Ms. Drew. Mr. Paley never sees anyone without an appointment." The secretary turned to her typewriter as if the matter were settled.

Just then, the door of Paley's office opened, and out stepped Jack Paley.

"Marian, this letter is—" He stopped when he saw Nancy. His eyes narrowed.

"Now, see here, young lady. I've had just about enough of your rudeness for one day." Jack Paley sounded almost as angry as he had earlier. "You have no right barging in here bothering my secretary——"

"Look, Mr. Paley," Nancy broke in. "I think you ought to know that we've just had another dangerous prank at Danner and Bishop."

"So what?" Mr. Paley said. "I'm a busy man. I don't have time to hear about every little problem you people run into over there."

Nancy took a deep breath. "Mr. Paley, why are you trying to ruin Danner and Bishop? Are you threatened by the competition?"

To Nancy's surprise, Jack Paley burst out laughing. "Young lady, Paley's department stores have been around for four generations. We have branches all over the country. One small store like Danner and Bishop is no threat to me!"

"Perhaps you're trying to lower the store's selling price, so that you could buy it more cheaply from Carlin Fitzhugh." Nancy challenged Paley with a stare.

The store owner gave Nancy a long, steady look. "Well, I'll say this for you—you have an awful lot of determination. I admire that. So I'm going to be honest with you.

"I have nothing—I repeat, nothing—to do with the pranks that are happening at Danner and Bishop. You're right, I do have an interest in buying the store. So it wouldn't make any sense for me to try to ruin the place, would it?"

Nancy had to admit that he had a point. But she wasn't totally convinced about his innocence yet. "What about Tom—"

"My son," Jack Paley interrupted her, "has a lot of problems. As I'm sure you could see this morning, we don't have a very good relationship. And he has been in trouble for shoplifting. He was in the store this morning—what he could possibly want there is beyond me—but he has nothing to do with the jokes."

Nancy still wasn't sure that the Paley family didn't have some hand in the mystery, but she knew she had stayed long enough at Paley's. Her break was almost over, and, in any case, she knew she wouldn't get any more information out of the store owner.

Nancy thanked Jack Paley and his secretary and quickly exited the store. On her way back, she thought over a few ideas.

When she reached Danner and Bishop, she walked through the main entrance still deep in thought. After a few moments, she realized that something was terribly wrong.

The main floor was a complete mess. Broken glass and merchandise were scattered every-where. People were wandering about aimlessly, some of them screaming or crying. The cosmetics counters glittered with shards of glass under the soft pink store lighting.

Nancy saw that customers were being led away from the scene by the security staff. Maintenance crews were already cleaning up the mess with brooms and vacuum cleaners.

"Welcome back, Nancy," George said dryly, appearing beside her. "This looks like a major disaster, doesn't it?"

"What happened, George?" Nancy said, staring.

"All of a sudden, a cosmetics display just exploded—metal, wood, and broken mirrors went flying everywhere. The panic was even worse. It was a real nightmare."

Nancy moved carefully among the debris, surveying the scene. She noticed some paramedics taking care of a few of the customers. Ann Fitzhugh was standing nearby, her arm around an ashen-faced woman. She was speaking gently to the woman, trying to calm her down.

"I overheard the doctor telling Ann that nobody had been seriously hurt," George whispered to Nancy.

"Thank goodness for that," Nancy said.

But even though there had been only minor injuries, it was clear to Nancy that Danner and Bishop's business had been hurt badly by this latest disaster. She listened to the customers complaining. Many of them were declaring that they would never shop at Danner and Bishop again.

"I can't believe it!" Nancy heard a woman in a fur coat say. "Imagine not being safe in a store like this!"

"Do you know," her companion said, "I heard that just yesterday there was an incident in the shoe department. A display fell over. I heard three people had to be hospitalized!"

"Well," said the first woman, "Mildred told me that when she was here last Saturday a chandelier fell down in the dress department! I think it's time to close my account with Danner and Bishop. From now on I buy at Paley's!"

All of this was playing right into the joker's hands, Nancy thought, looking around at the wreckage and the upset clientele.

Nancy's thoughts were interrupted by Nick Holt, who was sweeping up nearby. "Why hasn't security caught this joker yet?" he demanded when he saw Nancy.

"We're trying, Nick," Nancy answered.

"Frankly," Nick said in an annoyed tone, "I don't think Joe Dane is trying hard enough."

"I'm sure Joe is doing everything he can," Nancy said, remembering to act like an employee loyal to her boss.

The mention of Joe Dane reminded Nancy of

the matchbook that had fallen out of his pocket the day before. She had been so busy with the Paley connection, she hadn't had a chance to follow up on Omni Aviation yet. It seemed as if this would be a good time to make that call.

Nancy headed for the pay phones near the elevators and was surprised when Nick Holt followed her. He looked nervous and worried.

"I wasn't making any accusations against Joe or anything, you understand," he said as he trailed along beside Nancy. "Really, I was just asking."

Nancy stopped and faced Nick. "You seem awfully nervous, Nick. Is something wrong?"

"No, not really." He grinned sheepishly. "It's just that, well, Joe is a big guy, you know. I wouldn't want him to find out I was accusing him of anything."

"Don't worry," Nancy said with a laugh. "Your secret is safe with me. Now, if you don't mind, Nick, I have to make a phone call."

"Oh, sure. Go ahead," Nick said.

Nancy smiled at him and turned to the phone. She dialed the number for Omni Aviation. While she waited for someone to pick up at the other end, Nancy noticed that Nick was still standing nearby, in front of an elevator.

A woman's voice answered the phone with a cheery greeting. "Omni Aviation. Trish Jenner here. Can I help you?"

71

"I hope so," Nancy said. "May I speak with the manager or the person in charge?"

"I'm the owner. Is that in charge enough for you?" Trish Jenner chuckled.

"Great. My name is Nancy Drew, and I'm hoping you can give me some information. It's very important."

"Sounds serious." Trish Jenner's voice was warm and friendly. Nancy hoped she would be willing to give out some information.

Nancy glanced at Nick Holt, who was still hanging around nearby, and wondered if he was eavesdropping on her conversation. She didn't know what interest Nick could have in her phone call. He might simply be waiting for the elevator. But just to be careful, Nancy kept her voice low when she turned back to the phone.

"I need to know if your company has done any business lately with a man named Joe Dane."

"I know we haven't," Trish Jenner answered. "We don't handle personal accounts. We only deal with corporations."

"I see," Nancy said in a disappointed voice. She thought for a moment, then asked, "Well, can you tell me if you've had any dealings with Danner and Bishop?"

"Oh, yes," Trish Jenner said promptly. "Someone from the store just rented a helicopter in the name of Danner and Bishop."

A helicopter! Nancy felt a rush of excitement. Now she was getting somewhere. "Will you tell me who rented it?" Nancy asked eagerly.

"I'm sorry, that's confidential," Trish Jenner said. "I wish I could help you, but I can't give out any more information."

"I understand," Nancy said. "But maybe if I explain the situation to you, you'll change your mind." Then she explained that she was a detective working undercover at Danner and Bishop. She told the owner of Omni Aviation all about the pranks at Danner and Bishop and about the people hurt by the flying glass.

"All of us are in danger," Nancy finished. "That's why it's so important for me to find out who rented the helicopter and why. It may have something to do with the mystery."

When Nancy had finished speaking, there was a brief silence on the line. Then Trish Jenner said, "I'd like to help you, but I don't know if I can."

"Any information you could give me would help," Nancy said desperately. "A name, a destination, anything."

Nancy became aware of Nick Holt again. Now he was staring at her. Nancy wondered why he wasn't busy with the rest of the maintenance staff cleaning up the glass. She hoped he couldn't hear what she was saying.

"I don't know. I'll have to think about it," Trish Jenner finally said. "I'll check my files and get back to you."

"No, I'll call *you*," Nancy said. "And thank you."

Nancy hung up. Then she moved to the store phone and dialed the extension of Mr. Fitzhugh's secretary.

"Grace, this is Nancy Drew," Nancy said when the secretary answered the phone. "Do you know if anyone from Danner and Bishop has opened a corporate account with Omni Aviation?"

"Just a minute, Nancy," said Grace. "I'll check with Mark Hoffman. He's the one who handles those accounts."

Nancy waited impatiently. Out of the corner of her eye, she watched Nick Holt.

After a few minutes, Grace came back on the line. "Nancy? As far as Mark knows, no one from Danner and Bishop has ever rented a helicopter."

"Thanks, Grace," said Nancy. She hung up and bit her lip thoughtfully. She decided it was time to talk to Joe Dane. He would obviously be able to shed some light on the helicopter business. She walked over to Nick Holt.

"By the way, have you seen Joe?" she asked.

"Joe? Yeah, I saw him heading for the basement a little while ago," Nick said.

"Thanks," Nancy said and started to walk

74

away. She wondered if Nick would follow her again, and she was relieved when he didn't.

Bennett Lloyd had forgotten to show Nancy the basement when he gave her a tour of the store. When she got down there, Nancy found herself in a maze of long, shadowy corridors. The hallways were really a series of narrow ramps. The ceiling in the basement was low, with pipes just overhead.

Nancy walked down one of the hallways looking for Joe Dane.

"Joe?" she called tentatively. "Joe, are you down here?"

She turned a corner and started down another steep ramp. But she soon stopped when she found that the corridor came to a dead end.

"Great going, Nancy," she said out loud. She turned to walk back the way she had come.

But the passageway was blocked. It took Nancy a moment to realize that it was an enormous iron dolly filled with metal cabinets that was blocking her way out.

But the dolly wasn't just standing at the end of the corridor. It was zooming down the ramp out of control, racing straight at her!

Nancy was trapped, hemmed in on all sides. There was no way out.

8

Trapped!

The gigantic cart hurtled faster and faster toward
her. Nancy knew that unless she did something,
it would only be a matter of seconds before her
body was smashed into the wall.

She jumped up and grabbed one of the low-
hanging pipes. Using all her strength, Nancy
pulled her body up and over the pipes until she
was almost flat against the ceiling. She breathed
deeply and held on tight.

The iron dolly whizzed by, only inches below
her. It crashed into the wall Nancy had been
standing against with such force that all of the
pipes shook. The corridor rang with a loud
metallic sound.

Shaking with relief, Nancy slowly exhaled.

Although she had only been holding on to the pipe for a few seconds, her arms ached from the intensity of her grip. She slowly began to let herself down from the ceiling.

"Nancy!" George's voice sounded far away, echoing against the walls of the basement.

"I'm over here, George," Nancy yelled back. She was both surprised and glad to hear that her friend was nearby.

"I heard that crash." George's voice was getting closer. "Are you all right?"

George appeared at the corner as she finished speaking. She stared in disbelief at the smashed dolly and wall. George could see how great the force of the crash must have been to have caused so much damage.

"Oh, Nancy," George cried.

"It's okay, George," Nancy said, landing on the ground and starting to dust herself off. "I'm all in one piece. But I'm thinking about wearing a crash helmet from now on." She managed to grin at her friend. Then she said, "How did you know I was down here?"

"I saw you talking on the phone. Then you disappeared into the elevator. I saw the floor indicator read "B" for basement, so I figured that's where you'd gone."

"Come on," Nancy said. "Let's get out of here and go find Bess."

Upstairs the girls found their friend in a quiet

corner of the shoe department stockroom, taking a break.

Bess's blue eyes opened wide in shock when she heard about Nancy's latest near disaster.

"That's it," Bess sputtered. "I think it's time we got out of this store. It's too dangerous here. Let's just get out and leave this practical joker to the police."

"We can't just leave now, Bess," Nancy said patiently. "We're too close to solving this thing."

"Close?" Bess demanded. "Closer to being killed, maybe."

"Don't worry, Bess," Nancy said. "I've got some ideas. I think we'll be able to wrap up this case soon."

"What kind of ideas?" George asked.

"I'm starting to wonder about Lindy Dixon, for one thing," Nancy said. "Two of the pranks have taken place in the shoe department. She would have had plenty of opportunity to pull them off."

"That's true," George said slowly. "There was the falling display case and the itching powder."

"Right," Nancy agreed. "But some of the pranks are too complex for Lindy to have carried out. The falling light fixture in the cafeteria and the escalator—that's pretty fancy tampering. If Lindy *is* the prankster, she isn't working alone."

"And you have an idea of who her partner might be, don't you?" George said.

Nancy arched an eyebrow. "Joe Dane, maybe.

Or Nick Holt, who seems suspicious of Joe. He could be trying to frame Joe."

"And what about Mr. Paley and his son?" Bess asked. "You went to see him this afternoon, didn't you?"

Nancy sighed. "Jack Paley is someone to watch. It seems a little too convenient that the Danner and Bishop customers are leaving the store—and probably heading across town to Paley's."

"So what you're saying, Nancy, is that you have a lot of suspects, right?" Bess said.

"Okay, let's have it, Nancy," George said. "We know you have a theory by now."

"Well, there must be more than one Danner and Bishop insider involved," Nancy said thoughtfully. "Jack Paley may be the mastermind, but there have to be at least two people actually causing the pranks here in the store.

"If Trish Jenner at Omni Aviation comes through with some information," Nancy continued, "maybe that will give us a clue to which suspect is the joker." She shook her head. "But I really can't figure out why someone from the store would secretly rent a—"

Nancy stopped speaking abruptly when she noticed Lindy Dixon approaching. Lindy smiled at the girls and directed her attention to Bess.

"Oh, here you are, Bess," she said cheerfully. "Haven't you spent enough time chatting with your friends? I have a lot of work for you to do."

"What is it this time?" Bess asked wearily.

"It's those boxes all over the floor." Lindy's bracelets jangled as she pushed her long red hair over her shoulder. "This mess simply won't do— not at Danner and Bishop. We run a class act here, you know. Will you please stack all those boxes and put them away in the stockroom?" Lindy smiled brightly at Bess.

"Sure." Bess stood up, and, as Lindy turned and walked away, she rolled her eyes toward the ceiling. Before she followed her boss out to the selling floor, Bess whispered to her friends, "When Lindy gets to Broadway, her first role should be the wicked stepmother in Cinderella!"

Nancy and George burst out laughing.

"Lindy is going to be leaving early today for an audition," Bess told her friends. "So you guys can stay back here for a while if you want. You won't be bothering anybody."

Nancy and George took advantage of their next break time to meet in the stockroom and talk about Nancy's theory. They went over the list of suspects again and again, hoping to come up with some new clue or evidence they might have missed. Bess walked back and forth from the selling floor to the stockroom with the shoes that had been lying around the shoe department. After a while, Lindy came back in to get her big purple bag, and the girls heard her calling a cheerful goodbye to Bess.

"Well, I think this is the last of them," Bess announced a few minutes later as she walked into the stockroom carrying a huge pile of shoe boxes. "I can't wait—"

Bess never got to finish what she was saying. At that moment, the metal security door at the stockroom entrance slammed shut. Then the girls heard a bolt snapping into place with a loud click.

Someone was locking them in!

Nancy rushed to the door and tried to open it. She rattled the knob, but nothing happened. Then she and George slammed against the door with their shoulders. But the heavy iron door wouldn't budge.

Nancy turned to her friends in silence. Horror was mirrored on their faces as the girls realized they were trapped. They were locked in a remote back stockroom where no one would be likely to find them.

"Help! Someone help us!" Bess started screaming.

Nancy and George banged on the walls. After a few minutes they began to scream for help, too. Nancy knew that it was nearly closing time at the store. Soon only the attack dogs would be around to hear their screams.

Then something happened. "Shh!" Nancy said.

The girls suddenly froze in silence. They heard a muffled noise from outside.

"Someone heard us," Bess cried joyfully. "We're saved!" She rushed to the door and waited for it to open.

But the door remained solidly locked. A small sheet of paper was slipped under the door. Nancy reached down to pick it up. She gasped when she saw that it was a joker card.

The jester leered up at her, grinning like something out of a horror film.

Then the girls heard something that made their blood go icy cold.

From the other side of the locked door they heard a laugh—a low, evil, cruel laugh.

9

Under Stock and Key

The girls huddled together in silence. George and Bess looked at Nancy, hoping she would know what to do next.

Bess was the first to break the silence.

"I can't stand this!" Bess rattled the doorknob. "What are we going to do?" she cried.

"Bess, please calm down," Nancy said. "Getting hysterical isn't going to help us any. We'll get out of here soon enough."

"How?" Bess demanded. "It's almost closing time for the store, and nobody knows we're in here. We'll be stuck all night long!"

"Nancy's right, Bess," George said. "You've got to get a hold of yourself. Let's all try to look for another way out of here."

"I know this place," Bess told her friends after they had searched the stockroom thoroughly. "There is no other way out. We're prisoners in here!"

"Listen," Nancy said. "Don't forget about the Fitzhughs. When we don't show up at the mansion tonight, they'll start to worry."

"That's right," George said soothingly to Bess. "They're bound to come looking for us."

That seemed to work. Bess closed her eyes in relief. "You're right," she admitted. "I forgot about the Fitzhughs."

"I'm sure about one thing," Nancy said. "Lindy is definitely a prime suspect now. She's the only one who knew we were all in here."

"But that laugh, Nan." George shuddered as she remembered it. "That was a man's voice."

"It seemed to be," Nancy said, her eyes starting to roam around the room inspecting it carefully again. "But don't forget that Lindy's an actress. She might be able to change her voice. Or she could be working with a man—I'm beginning to think there's more than one jester."

Nancy sat down. "It looks as if we're going to be in here for a while. So we might as well make ourselves comfortable."

The girls sat, talking quietly, for several hours.

"You realize, don't you, that the store closed ages ago," Bess said finally as she looked at her watch.

84

"So there's no one around," George said brave-ly. "No problem. The Fitzhughs will find us eventually."

"Wait a minute." Bess looked worried. "Do you remember what the security staff uses to patrol the store at night?"

There was a moment of grim silence as the girls realized what Bess meant.

"The Dobermans," Nancy said.

"The *killer* Dobermans," Bess said emphatical-ly. "Prowling around at night, ready to attack!"

"Don't worry about it, Bess," said George. "Somehow I don't think they're smart enough to open the stockroom door!" She looked at Nancy, who was staring up at the ceiling.

"What is it, Nancy?" George asked.

"Look at that," Nancy said, pointing. Bess and George heard the excitement in her voice. "The cover on that ventilator. If we could get the cover off, I bet I could crawl through the airshaft. I might be able to get to the selling floor."

"You're right!" George exclaimed. "Do you think those shelves are sturdy enough to work as a ladder?"

"Let's find out," Nancy replied. She stepped onto the first shelf, gripped the sides, and pulled herself up a little.

"I think this will work," she said.

"But, Nancy," Bess said, "what about the Dobermans?"

The girls' eyes met. Nancy knew it was a risk she would have to take. "I wouldn't be a good detective if I couldn't outsmart a couple of dogs, would I?" Her calm voice, masking her own doubts, raised Bess's spirits.

Nancy opened her purse and pulled out her Swiss Army knife. She climbed the shelves, and, with George supporting her from below, she began to loosen the vent cover with her knife. It didn't take long to remove it.

"Nancy, take this flashlight," Bess said. "We keep it here for emergencies, and I think this situation qualifies."

"Thanks," Nancy said, sticking it in her back pocket.

Nancy squeezed into the airshaft. She found herself looking into the yawning opening of a dark, narrow hole.

"I'm on my way," Nancy called to her friends.

The airshaft was dark and dirty. As Nancy crawled along on her hands and knees, she felt cobwebs brushing by her face.

Nancy moved forward for about fifty feet before she came to a long, narrow, vertical shaft. It seemed to go all the way from the top floor to the basement.

Staring down the airshaft in the dim light, Nancy could barely see a ladder attached to one side of the wall. When she reached out to touch it, Nancy felt rough edges of rusted metal against her palm.

The ladder was loose and unstable, but Nancy knew she had no other choice. Carefully, she placed one foot on a rung. The ladder creaked and swayed.

Slowly Nancy began to climb down. So far, so good, she thought.

Suddenly, the metal rung Nancy was gripping broke loose. She grabbed for another rung but lost her balance.

She made another desperate grab, but the ladder seemed to be out of reach.

Nancy felt herself falling. She groped wildly in the dark, knowing that the ladder had to be there somewhere. She was careening down into the black hole, the rough walls of the airshaft scraping at her clothes and skin. She had to break her fall before she picked up too much speed.

Finally, she managed to grab at something that felt like a rung. Nancy gripped tightly and managed to get her footing.

She was back on the ladder!

She paused for a second to catch her breath. Her heart was beating wildly, and her breath came in heavy gasps. Her arms were sore from the effort of stopping her fall. But Nancy knew she had to keep going. She started to climb down again.

Finally, Nancy made it to the first floor, where she found another horizontal crawl space like the one on the third floor.

Here we go again, she thought grimly, plunging into the opening.

She didn't have to travel far before she came to a hole in the airshaft. She looked down and saw light.

Nancy's heart skipped a beat. She was looking down at the cosmetics department where the display counters had exploded earlier in the day!

Nancy squeezed carefully through the hole and jumped to the ground, near the handbag counter. She stood for a few seconds, brushing the dirt from her clothes. Then she pulled out the flashlight and played its beam around the dimly lit floor.

The next instant, Nancy heard a sound behind her that made her freeze in her tracks—the snarl of a dog! She spun around and was greeted with two ferocious barks.

A huge, sleek Doberman stood in the shadows before her, ready to attack.

Nancy swallowed hard and then said, "Nice boy," in a voice she hoped was calm and soothing. "Nice boy . . ."

She backed away slowly, wondering if she could somehow escape the dog. If only she could move slowly toward the elevators behind the lipstick counter . . .

But the Doberman was too well trained. With a vicious growl, the dog made a powerful leap toward Nancy!

Nancy turned and ran, but the dog was faster than she could ever be. It caught up with her easily and made a savage grab at her pants' cuff. Nancy could feel the dog's hot breath on her leg as its teeth tore at the fabric.

Nancy threw the flashlight at the dog, trying to startle it into letting her go. The flashlight hit the huge dog's paw and bounced to the floor. The dog didn't even flinch.

Nancy tried desperately to break away from the dog's razorlike teeth.

Nancy stumbled to her knees. A second later, the monstrous dog jumped on her back and knocked her to the ground.

Nancy had run out of ideas. She looked up into the snarling, hideous mouth of the angry animal. She knew the next few seconds might be her last.

10

Joe Dane's Story

Nancy's body was rigid, braced for the horrible pain that she knew would be coming. She and the dog stared at each other. Nancy knew that there was nothing more she could do. She was trapped.

"Heel, Marcus!" The command came from a deep, authoritative voice booming out from the shadows. The dog loosened its hold on Nancy's leg.

"Heel!" the voice repeated. Obediently, the dog turned and ran toward the voice.

Nancy went limp with relief. She peered into the darkness, trying to see who had saved her.

A tall, heavyset figure moved toward her. Nancy looked up and recognized Joe Dane, the head of store security.

Dane frowned when he saw Nancy. "What are you doing here?" he growled. "This isn't your shift."

Nancy got to her feet. She looked first at Joe, then at the vicious Doberman he was holding by the collar. If Joe Dane were the prankster, she could be in even more danger than she had been before. But she had to take her chances. Quickly she explained how she, Bess, and George had been trapped in the stockroom.

Joe Dane seemed startled by the news and quickly locked up the Doberman. Together they started walking to the third-floor shoe department.

Nancy used the opportunity to question her official boss. "How is it that you're here at this hour?"

"It's my job to be here," Joe answered in his deep, gruff voice. "Somebody on the security staff always works the night shift with these dogs."

Nancy nodded. She knew some of the security staff was specially trained to handle the Dobermans.

"I've had this shift ever since the pranks started," Dane added. "I chose it on purpose. I thought it might be a good opportunity to get to the bottom of this problem."

Joe Dane sounded sincere, but Nancy wasn't sure whether to believe him or not. He could easily have chosen the night shift to set up the pranks.

As if he had read her thoughts, Joe said, "I'm convinced this guy is setting up his practical jokes at night." He shook his head. "But he must be too smart for me. I haven't been able to catch him."

The frustrated tone in Joe's voice sounded real enough. Nancy suddenly remembered what Nick Holt had said to her about Joe Dane.

"Has the trouble with the practical jokes put your job on the line, Joe?" Nancy asked.

He stopped walking and stared at her for a moment. Then he gave a genuine laugh of amusement. "No way. Carlin Fitzhugh is my cousin."

"I didn't know that," Nancy said in a surprised voice.

"Sure! We're family, and Carlin is very protective of his family. He'd never fire me. In fact, he's got at least a dozen relatives who work at the store."

Nancy wondered if Nick Holt knew that Joe and Carlin Fitzhugh were cousins. If he *did* know, then why had he lied to her about Joe's job being on the line?

Joe added, "Frankly, I think Carlin's got the right attitude. He's been really good to me. I'd do anything to help him out."

Again, Nancy was struck by the sincere note in Joe's voice. But she wasn't ready to believe his story. Not yet. They were close to the shoe department now. She only had time for one more question.

"Joe," Nancy said slowly. "What do you know about Omni Aviation?"

Joe's big, square face suddenly turned red. Nancy was surprised to see the expression of alarm that lit up his eyes. He picked up his pace.

"Where did you hear about that?" he asked.

Nancy paused for a moment. Then she replied truthfully, "I saw it on a matchbook that dropped out of your pocket the other day. I picked it up near the elevator."

"I was wondering what happened to that. It was my only clue!" Joe shook his head in frustration. "I was positive it was connected with the pranks somehow."

"Where did it come from?" Nancy asked.

"Well," Joe said grudgingly, "since you're on the security staff, I guess I should tell you.

"About a week and a half ago, I was patrolling outside the employee cafeteria about half an hour after the store had closed. I overheard some people talking, and I couldn't help listening. They were talking about Danner and Bishop being ruined. They were saying that Carlin Fitzhugh deserved to go to the poorhouse. They sounded really bitter."

"Who were they?" Nancy asked.

"That's just it," Joe said. "I couldn't see them without them seeing me. I didn't want anyone to know that I was listening to them. They were talking so low that I couldn't recognize their voices."

"Could you tell how many of them were there?" Nancy asked.

"It sounded like a man and a woman. Maybe two men. I can't be sure."

"Well, what else did they say?" Nancy wanted to know.

"They said they were going to rent something and that it was really expensive—two hundred fifty dollars an hour. They didn't mention exactly what it was they were renting, but one of the men said something about the price being 'sky high.' That phrase stuck in my mind because the others told him to stop joking around."

Nancy nodded, taking everything in.

Joe went on, "I wanted to find out who these people were, so I walked around to the other entrance to the cafeteria. But by the time I got there, they had left. I picked up the matchbook that was left on the table, thinking it might be a clue. I thought I might find someone using the same matches. Then watch who he or she hangs around with."

"I think you're right about that," Nancy said, nodding. "I called Omni Aviation and found out that someone from Danner and Bishop has rented a helicopter."

Joe's mouth dropped open in amazement. "A helicopter?"

"It ties in with the sky-high joke you heard," Nancy commented.

"But why would anyone want to rent a helicopter?"

"It would make a great getaway vehicle," Nancy pointed out. "But who's trying to get away? And from where?"

Nancy realized that Joe Dane couldn't possibly be the joker. It seemed very unlikely that he would have made up the story about what he had heard in the cafeteria. The helicopter was definitely something the culprits wanted to keep secret.

Finally, they reached the stockroom door. Nancy wasted no time in calling out to her trapped friends. "George! Bess! We're here! You'll be out of there in no time!"

Joe unbolted the lock. The door flew open, and Bess and George came rushing out.

"We're free!" Bess cried.

"Are we glad to see you!" George exclaimed.

Suddenly Bess clutched Nancy's arm. "What about the dogs?" she asked in a hushed voice.

"Don't worry," Nancy reassured her. "If we come across one on this floor, Joe will handle him." She smiled to herself. It was a good thing Bess hadn't come with her through the airshaft.

"Let's get out of here," Bess suggested. "I've had enough of this store for one day."

"I'll walk you to the back door," Joe said. "I don't want anything else happening to you to-night."

"Let's get together first thing tomorrow morning," Nancy suggested to Joe when they got to the back door. "If we work with each other on this, we should be able to come up with some answers soon."

"Good idea." Joe lifted his wrist to look at his watch. "Is nine o'clock okay?"

"Fine," Nancy answered. "I'll meet you at the front entrance."

"That's a great watch, Joe," George said.

Joe held out his wrist to give the girls a closer look. They all admired the beautiful, expensive-looking gold watch.

"I'd love to buy one like that for my dad," George said.

"You won't find many like this," Joe said. "It's very expensive and rare. It was a special gift to me from Carlin Fitzhugh on my twentieth anniversary with Danner and Bishop."

Nancy smiled. There was a great deal of pride and affection in Joe's voice. Nancy knew he had meant what he had said earlier. Joe Dane *was* willing to do anything for Carlin Fitzhugh. As she said good night to Joe, Nancy felt she could scratch one suspect from her list.

The next morning at nine o'clock, Nancy was waiting at the store entrance for Joe. She planned to ask him to go with her to Omni Aviation. Trish Jenner might be more willing to open up in front of the head of store security. Then she wanted to question Nick Holt and Lindy Dixon.

Nancy was starting to get impatient at 9:10, when Joe hadn't arrived yet. By 9:20, she was annoyed. At 9:30, she started to worry.

Finally, at ten o'clock, Nancy couldn't wait any longer. She found Ann Fitzhugh and got Joe Dane's address and phone number.

She tried calling him first, but there was no answer.

Then, armed with a map of Chicago, she got her sports car out of the employee lot and headed for Joe's small house on the outskirts of the city. Nancy parked in front of the house and looked up the walk. She was surprised to find the front door wide open.

Cautiously, Nancy walked through the doorway. "Joe?" she called out. The place seemed to be deserted. "Joe?" she called again.

Nancy walked through the hall into the living room. She spotted an overturned chair, and her stomach tensed.

She stood still and took in the scene before her.

Lamps had been knocked to the floor, and the phone cord had been pulled out of the wall. A cold breeze whipped in through an open window.

Nancy searched through the rest of the house; but it was no use. Joe was gone.

As she turned to leave, she noticed something familiar lying halfway under the open front door—a joker card. Joe Dane had been kidnapped!

11

Closing In on the Joker

Nancy ran out of the house, jumped into her car, and headed back to Danner and Bishop. As soon as she stepped into the store, she bumped into Nick Holt. He was at the top of her list of suspects now. Was he responsible for Joe Dane's disappearance?

"Hey there, Nancy," Nick said cheerfully.

"Hi, Nick," replied Nancy. She noticed a nasty cut over Nick's eye. "Is that painful?" she asked, pointing to the cut.

"Oh, that." Nick paused, his cheerful mood quickly fading. "That's nothing."

"How did it happen?"

Nick seemed annoyed by Nancy's questions. "I got it yesterday when we were cleaning up that broken glass in the cosmetics department," he said.

"Really?" Nancy found his explanation difficult to believe, but she was worried that if she pushed him too far she'd scare him off. If he was on his guard right now, he was unlikely to let anything slip. If she wanted to find out if Nick knew about Joe Dane, she'd have to pick a different moment. "Well, I guess I'd better get to work," Nancy said casually. "See you later."

"Yeah, right," Nick said. Nancy noticed that he looked relieved.

Nancy headed toward the shoe department. Lindy was the next person Nancy wanted to question. Lindy seemed to be the most likely person to have locked the girls in the stockroom the night before. Nancy could try to talk to her about that, not letting the actress know that she was concerned about Joe. Joe's safety was the most important thing on Nancy's mind. She knew she couldn't take any risks while he was in jeopardy.

When Nancy reached the third floor, she was glad to see everything was quiet in the shoe department. There were no exploding countertops, no falling display cases, and no itching shoes.

"Bess." Nancy quietly approached her friend. "Is Lindy around?"

Bess made a face. "She called in sick today, so I

have to handle the whole department by myself. Can you believe it?"

"I believe it. This thing is starting to get out of control." Nancy sighed. "Bess, listen. Joe Dane is missing."

"Missing? What do you mean missing?"

"I went to his house and he wasn't there," Nancy said. "I think he's been kidnapped!"

"Well, I think all this detective stuff is starting to affect your brain," Bess said with her hands on her hips. "Just because he's not home doesn't mean he's missing or that he's been kidnapped."

"It does when the door is left wide open and all of the furniture has been tossed around looking as if there's been some sort of a fight," Nancy told her friend. "And there was one other thing—a joker card."

"Oh." Bess gulped. "Nancy, what are you going to do?"

Nancy thought for a moment. "I guess I should report back to the Fitzhughs and tell them about Joe. I'll let them report the break-in at Joe's house. Then I want to follow up on Omni Aviation," Nancy said.

"Good idea," Bess agreed. "The sooner we can solve this case, the better. I really want to get out of this store!"

Nancy smiled sympathetically at her friend and then went to the store phone. She called Carlin Fitzhugh and told him everything that had happened. The store owner was very concerned about his cousin.

"I'll do my best to find him," Nancy told Mr. Fitzhugh. "But I think you should be prepared to call the police."

Carlin Fitzhugh agreed reluctantly.

Nancy hung up. Then she moved to the pay phone. She pulled the matchbook from her purse and dialed the number for Omni Aviation.

"Hello, Ms. Jenner?" Nancy decided to keep her conversation with the company owner as friendly and informal as possible. "It's Nancy Drew again. Any information on the Danner and Bishop helicopter rental?"

"Oh . . . hi, Ms. Drew." Trish Jenner sounded friendly but hesitant. "There are some customers here right now. I really don't have time to talk."

"Can I come out to the airport to speak with you?" Nancy asked. "I promise I won't take much of your time."

"Um . . . yes, okay."

"Great," Nancy said and hung up. She hoped she might finally be on to something. She also hoped that Trish Jenner would be willing to talk.

As Nancy headed out to the airport, her mind was filled with worries about Joe Dane.

What was the joker going to do with him? Nancy wondered. She could only hope that he hadn't been hurt. Either way, she had to move *fast.*

102

At the airport, Nancy pushed thoughts of Joe out of her mind when she found the Omni Aviation building.

A long cluttered desk took up most of the reception room that Nancy entered. Sitting behind the desk was a pretty black woman in her mid-thirties. She looked up at Nancy and said, "Hi, can I help you?"

"Hi," Nancy said with a smile. "Are you Trish Jenner?"

"Yes." The woman looked at Nancy carefully. "And I'll bet you're Nancy Drew." Nancy nodded. "Well, come on in. Have a seat."

"Thanks, Ms. Jenner," Nancy said, sitting in front of Trish Jenner's desk.

"Call me Trish," the woman said with a smile. "You're much younger than I expected. You don't seem old enough to be a detective," Trish added teasingly.

"Well, I *am* eighteen, and I've been doing this for a while," Nancy said. "I've solved quite a few cases. But I'm really worried about this one. It's stumping me. That's why I'm hoping you'll give me some information."

"I'll be happy to help you in any way I can," said Trish. Her smile widened. "You see, I called Mr. Fitzhugh at Danner and Bishop about you."

Nancy returned Trish's smile. "That was good detective work."

Trish bent down over some papers. "Now,

where did I put that file?" She flipped through the clutter on her desk. "Oh, here it is."

Trish scanned through the file. "Well, I'm afraid there's not much to go on here. According to these papers, the helicopter was rented by—would you believe it?—Jane Smith. She showed me a company ID, too. She said she represented the store."

Nancy was sure the ID card was a fake. The name was probably phony, too. Mark Hoffman in Danner and Bishop's corporate accounts had said that nobody had rented anything from Omni Aviation.

"Do you remember when this 'Jane Smith' came in?" Nancy asked. "Can you describe her?"

"Oh, sure, I remember her," Trish said. "She was quite a character—young, lots of long dark frizzy hair, huge red sunglasses, and a thick Southern accent. How's that for a memory?"

"Terrific," Nancy said, trying to think of anyone who might fit that description. No one came to mind.

"Tell me, Trish," Nancy said. "Was there anything unusual about this woman?"

"Unusual?" Trish said in surprise. "I'm not sure what you mean. She was wearing a lot of makeup, I remember. And I thought her accent was too heavy—kind of exaggerated."

"Exaggerated like an actress playing a part?"

Nancy asked. She figured that Lindy could probably act the part easily.

"Could be," Trish said thoughtfully.

Nancy leaned forward. "Can you tell me anything more?" she asked Trish. "Like, when is the helicopter scheduled to be picked up and its destination?"

Trish turned her attention back to the file.

"This is strange," she commented. "This 'Jane Smith' said that she would call to tell me the exact time of pickup and the destination later. All she gave me was a date and an approximate time."

"When?" Nancy asked.

Trish looked into the file and said, "Tonight."

Tonight! Nancy thought in alarm. Something big was going to happen at Danner and Bishop that night, and Nancy still didn't know what it could be. If she didn't find out soon, the joker would be able to get away with whatever he or she was planning.

"Can you tell me anything else?"

"I'm sorry, Nancy," Trish said. "That's all I've got. I won't know any more until 'Jane Smith' gets in touch with me."

"Could I call you, Trish, throughout the day?" Nancy asked. "I want to find out what 'Jane Smith' has to say."

"Definitely. I feel as if I'm involved in this

thing now, too. I'll do whatever I can to help," Trish replied.

"Thanks, Trish," said Nancy as she got up to leave. "You've been great."

"Good luck, Nancy," Trish said sincerely. She waved goodbye as Nancy hurried off.

As soon as she got back to Danner and Bishop, Nancy headed for the maintenance department's locker room to find George.

"Anybody here?" Nancy called into the room.

Nobody answered, so Nancy turned to leave. But before the door swung closed behind her, Nancy thought she heard the scrape of metal inside.

Curious, she pushed the door open again and wandered farther into the room. Peeking around the rows of lockers, Nancy finally spotted Nick Holt standing in front of an open locker.

"Hi, Nick," Nancy said. "Just the guy I wanted to see. I need to ask you—"

"Not right now, Nancy," Nick said. He grabbed something out of his locker and stuffed it into a tote bag at his feet.

"This will just take a minute," Nancy said.

"No way. I'm late now." Nick looked down at his gold wristwatch and quickly slammed the locker shut. Before Nancy could say another word, he pushed past her and disappeared.

Nancy leaned against the lockers. Something

was bothering her about Nick. There was something more than his brisk manner that was wrong.

Nancy went over their short conversation in her mind. She tried to remember every movement Nick had made.

He had emptied his locker, closed his tote bag, and . . .

Then it hit her.

Nick Holt had been wearing Joe Dane's watch!

12

Computer Crash

Nancy knew there was no time to lose. She dashed out of the locker room and looked up and down the halls. Nick Holt was nowhere in sight.

Nancy ran to the selling floor and then slowed to a rapid walk, not wanting to attract attention.

She felt a shiver go through her body as she realized the danger Joe was in. Her hunch about Nick had been right—he had been involved all along, but he'd tried to throw suspicion on Joe. He'd hinted that Joe's job was in jeopardy, but he didn't know Fitzhugh and Joe were cousins.

Nancy walked through the store, asking every employee she ran into if they had seen Nick. But no one knew where he was. And something else made matters worse.

As Nancy worked her way through the now familiar store, she became more and more aware that Danner and Bishop was in deep trouble.

It wasn't an elegant, efficiently run store anymore. The employees seemed uneasy and distrustful—and Nancy couldn't blame them. The joker's pranks had made their jobs simply too dangerous.

And the store looked awful. Many of the once beautiful displays had been taken apart so they wouldn't be destroyed by the practical joker. The cosmetics counters still hadn't been repaired, and there was tape everywhere, holding things together. Nancy felt sorry for Carlin Fitzhugh as she walked through the aisles of the store. His beautiful Danner and Bishop was literally falling apart.

Nancy searched each floor thoroughly for Nick. When she reached the top floor, where the fur and fine jewelry were sold, Nancy stopped at the top of the escalator. Her eyes scanned the soft pink walls, white marble pillars, and plush carpeting.

There was something even stranger about the top floor, Nancy noticed immediately. Compared to the shabbiness in the other departments, the top floor was an oasis of calmness and elegance.

Nancy realized that this floor hadn't been hit by the prankster. It hadn't occurred to her before, but now she thought that it was odd. Why hadn't he struck here, where the most expensive items in the store were kept?

"That's odd," Nancy murmured to herself. If someone had wanted to do real damage to the store, it would make sense to harm the most valuable merchandise. But the jewelry lay neatly in the display counters, and the shining furs were in perfect order, hanging side by side along the mirrored walls.

Nancy bit her lip. She had a gut feeling that the untouched top floor could hold the key to the prankster puzzle.

The area was quiet now, and Nancy could see that Nick wasn't around, so she walked back downstairs. Nancy was more concerned than ever about Joe. She knew it was time to talk to Carlin Fitzhugh about calling the police.

Mr. Fitzhugh was out to lunch, his secretary told Nancy a few minutes later. Nancy was upset. She had wanted to tell him about the rented helicopter. It would be important, Nancy knew, for the Fitzhughs to be on their guard that night.

On impulse, Nancy headed toward Bennett Lloyd's tiny, windowless office. She didn't stop to knock but flung open the door and walked right in.

She was glad she had. Bennett Lloyd was hurriedly going through a desk drawer, a large Danner and Bishop shopping bag on the floor beside him. He was filling the bag with the contents of the desk.

"It looks as if you're leaving us, Mr. Lloyd," Nancy said quietly.

Bennett Lloyd turned and looked at Nancy. There was a brief flash of annoyance in his eyes, and then he laughed heartily. Nancy thought the laugh sounded forced.

"Me? Leave Danner and Bishop?" Mr. Lloyd chuckled. "No, it will be some years yet before that happens."

"Then why are you cleaning out your desk?" Nancy asked.

Mr. Lloyd sat down in the chair behind his desk and sighed deeply before answering.

"I'm tired, Nancy," he said. "All these practical jokes and all the confusion have exhausted me."

"Really?" Nancy raised her eyebrows innocently. "So you're clearing out your desk to relax yourself?"

"No." Bennett Lloyd smiled at her. "I've decided to take a vacation. My first one in ten years! I'm leaving tonight—for Hawaii."

"Isn't this a little sudden?" Nancy asked.

"Well, yes it is," answered Mr. Lloyd. "But I decided I needed a vacation *now*."

It wouldn't make sense for a store executive to leave town in the middle of a crisis, Nancy thought. "What airline are you taking?" she asked, hoping she seemed only casually curious.

"TransPacific Airways," Mr. Lloyd said calmly.

Nancy wasn't convinced that Mr. Lloyd was telling the truth. But she had to let someone know about her findings, and since she hadn't been able to talk to Mr. Fitzhugh, she decided to tell Bennett Lloyd.

"I think you ought to know that Joe Dane has disappeared," Nancy told him. "He didn't show up for work today. When I went out to his house to check on him, I found the place had been ransacked. There was a jester card planted by the doorway."

"Did you call the police?" Bennett Lloyd asked, looking concerned.

"Not yet," Nancy said. "There's more. I ran into Nick Holt, and I noticed that he was wearing Joe's wristwatch. I know Joe would never part with that watch—it was a gift from Mr. Fitzhugh."

Bennett Lloyd looked shocked. Nancy decided to go a little further and told him about being locked in the stockroom the night before and her suspicions about Lindy.

"This is the last straw," Bennett Lloyd said. "We've got to call the police. I'll tell you what, Nancy. I'll make the call while you continue searching for Nick. He's got to be in the store somewhere."

The store manager's plan made sense, so Nancy left Bennett Lloyd's office and headed down the hall. As she passed the computer room, she heard a voice cry out, "Oh no! We've crashed!"

Nancy hurried into the large room. "What's going on?" she asked the nearest person.

"Our screens all went blank!" the woman replied. "No one knows what's going on. I had a lot of sales information in front of me, and it just suddenly disappeared! The backup systems are failing, too! If those go, we'll lose all of our accounts!"

Everyone was talking at once. As far as Nancy could tell, it seemed as if the whole computer system had shut down all at once.

Someone called Bennett Lloyd, and a moment later he came rushing into the room. He began running from one terminal to the next, testing them all. Nancy watched as he pressed different combinations of buttons, but he was unable to bring up any of the lost information to the screens.

Still, the store manager kept at it, trying each machine. "We can't lose our sales information like this," he muttered to Nancy. "The store won't be able to function if our computer files have disappeared."

"Nothing is happening, Mr. Lloyd," one of the workers said. "The screens are still blank."

Bennett Lloyd looked up at Nancy, an expression of defeat on his face. "We've lost everything," he said in a dull voice. "This practical joker has finally wiped us out. All of our customer records are destroyed. The store will go bankrupt!"

Ann Fitzhugh came rushing into the computer room, looking pale and shaken.

"I called the technicians," she said. "But I have a feeling that we've lost all of our valuable information today."

She looked so sad that Nancy went over to her. "Maybe there's something we can do," Nancy said hopefully.

"Somehow I doubt it, Nancy," Ann whispered.

When the team of computer technicians arrived, it didn't take them long to come to an unhappy conclusion. The lost information was irretrievable.

"So the joker wins again," Ann said bleakly, turning away from the blank computer screens.

"Oh no!" she cried suddenly. "Not now." She turned back toward Nancy, an angry expression on her face.

"What is it?" Nancy asked, alarmed.

"Jack Paley. I just saw him down the hall."

Nancy turned and saw Mr. Paley striding toward them. She looked at Ann with a puzzled expression. "What's he doing here?"

"I don't know." Ann shrugged. "But it looks as if we're going to find out pretty soon."

Ann was right. A few moments later, Jack Paley was at the entrance to the computer room.

"Where's Carlin Fitzhugh?" he demanded.

"Why, hello, Mr. Paley. How are you?" Ann asked sweetly.

"Don't waste my time. I'm here to see Carlin Fitzhugh," Jack Paley said rudely.

"What do you want, Jack?" Mr. Fitzhugh asked, appearing behind him.

"We need to talk," Mr. Paley said.

"Well, why don't you step into my office," Carlin Fitzhugh suggested, and the two men moved away.

Ann, Nancy, and Bennett Lloyd looked at each other in confusion. "I don't know why Dad is willing to have anything to do with that horrible man," Ann said.

"Let's find out what Paley's doing here," Nancy suggested. The three of them crept to the door of Carlin Fitzhugh's office. They could hear angry voices inside.

"This is my final offer, Fitzhugh!" they heard Jack Paley shout.

"Forget it, you cheap crook," Carlin Fitzhugh growled back at him. "I'd rather go out of business than sell Danner and Bishop to you. Now, get out of my office!"

Nancy, Ann, and Bennett Lloyd backed away as Jack Paley came charging through the door. Nancy stared at Paley's retreating figure. She

115

couldn't help wondering why he had shown up just as the computer crisis had been happening. She still wasn't completely satisfied that Jack Paley had nothing to do with the pranks.

Jack Paley stormed down the hall to the elevators.

Carlin Fitzhugh came out of his office, looking angry. "Well?" he demanded of the three gathered outside his office. "I suppose a million other things are wrong here at the store. I suppose we're ruined by now. Who's going to fill me in on the latest?"

Bennett Lloyd checked his watch. "I'm afraid I've got to go, Mr. Fitzhugh. My plane leaves in several hours, and I must get home to finish packing."

"Packing!" Carlin Fitzhugh turned on Lloyd with fury. "You don't mean to tell me that you really plan to leave us in this big mess?"

"I'm afraid so." Bennett Lloyd looked tense. "I have these reservations for Hawaii, you see."

"You can't do this to me!" Fitzhugh blustered. "I need a manager now more than ever! My store is falling apart!"

"I'm sorry," Bennett Lloyd said shakily. "But this is my first vacation in years, and I need it."

"You can take a vacation later," Carlin Fitzhugh said. "First we've got to clean up the first floor and try to make some sense out of the computer mixup . . ."

"No," Bennett Lloyd said, shaking his head regretfully. "I have a ticket to Hawaii, and I'm not giving it up for anything."

Carlin Fitzhugh sputtered with indignation. "I thought I could count on you, Lloyd. After all these years . . ."

"Yes, Mr. Fitzhugh, after all these years when you have had many vacations. And I have had none!" Bennett Lloyd said. With that, he turned on his heel and left.

"What next?" Carlin Fitzhugh sighed wearily. "What could possibly happen next?"

"Well," said Nancy, "I can tell you what already has happened."

"What do you mean?" Ann asked.

"For one thing," Nancy began, "I'm really worried about Joe Dane."

Nancy told Ann and Carlin Fitzhugh about Nick and the watch.

"I can see why you're worried, Nancy," Mr. Fitzhugh said, a frown on his face. "I guess we'll have to get the police in on this."

"I'm afraid I haven't told you everything yet," Nancy said. She filled them in on her conversation with Trish Jenner.

"But what is the joker going to do here tonight with a helicopter?" Ann asked.

"I don't know," Nancy admitted. "Yet. But I'm going to find out. In fact, I should call Trish Jenner now and see if she's heard anything."

117

"Use the phone in my office, Nancy," Ann suggested.

"Thanks."

In Ann's office, Nancy dialed the Omni Aviation number. The line was busy. Nancy slammed down the receiver in frustration.

She picked it up again and called information for the TransPacific Airways number. Nancy knew that the airline wasn't likely to give out much information about their passengers, so when she spoke to the airline representative she made up a story.

"I'm Mr. Bennett Lloyd's personal secretary," she said in her most businesslike voice. "I'd like to confirm his reservation on this evening's flight to Hawaii. Mr. Lloyd would like a seat in the nonsmoking section."

"Just one moment, ma'am," the clerk said. "I'll check that for you."

Nancy was put on hold for a minute. When the clerk came back on the line, she was apologetic.

"I'm sorry, ma'am, but the computer shows no reservation for a Mr. Bennett Lloyd on the eight o'clock flight to Hawaii."

"No?" Nancy asked. "Well, maybe he's booked on another flight," she suggested.

"Oh, no," the clerk replied. "That's our only flight to Hawaii tonight."

"I see," Nancy said slowly. "Thank you. I'll check that out with Mr. Lloyd." She hung up the phone, her heart hammering. So Bennett Lloyd had lied to her.

Nancy wondered what the store manager was up to. He had certainly been packing as if he were planning to leave Danner and Bishop for good.

Nancy's thoughts were interrupted by a yell.

"Everybody out!" hollered a man's voice in the hallway. Curious, Nancy poked her head out of the office. People were running and pushing into the halls, heading for the emergency exits.

At first Nancy couldn't figure out what was going on, but then she saw it.

Thick, dark smoke was pouring into the hall from the air vents.

Then all the fire alarms in the store went off at once with a deafening sound.

"Everyone out of the store," the voice was still yelling as the crowd's panic grew.

"Nancy! Nancy!"

Nancy saw Ann Fitzhugh pushing through the crowd toward her. "Nancy, we have to get out! The building's on fire!"

13

Where There's Smoke . . .

Nancy followed Ann down the hall but quickly lost sight of her in the crowd of people. Nancy got caught up in the panicking mob pushing toward the stairway.

She allowed herself to be carried along by the flow of people, trying to sort out exactly what was happening. Her eyes began to tear as the smoke became thicker. People were coughing and choking.

Nancy reached the first floor just as the store's sprinkler systems were activated. Water came spitting and splashing down, adding to the panic. Customers were running to the front of the store, causing a jam of people by the revolving doors.

Several emergency exits were yawning open, and Nancy headed toward one of them.

"Bess!" Nancy yelled, spotting her friend in the crowd.

Bess turned, and her expression flooded with relief when she saw Nancy. "Talk about nightmares," she muttered when Nancy had caught up with her.

"Let's just get out of here," Nancy said, starting to cough from all the smoke.

The girls headed out of the store through a side exit. Gratefully, they breathed in the cold, clear air. When Nancy finally caught her breath, she turned to Bess with a look of deep concern. "Where's George? Have you seen her?"

Bess turned pale. "Oh no. Nancy, I don't see her anywhere!"

The two girls rushed through the milling groups of employees and customers but came up empty-handed. It was only after they returned to their original spot outside the store that George came up to them. The three girls huddled together away from the crowd.

"I can't believe this," Bess said. "I thought we had seen everything that could possibly go wrong in this store already. But a fire definitely tops them all!"

"Well, I'm not so sure there *is* a fire," Nancy said.

"What are you talking about, Nancy?" George asked.

"Of course there's a fire!" Bess exclaimed. "All those people were yelling, and there was all that smoke." Bess shuddered at the thought.

"But do you remember anyone actually saying they *saw* a fire?" Nancy asked calmly.

Bess was silent for a moment. "No, I don't. The smoke was so thick, I don't think anybody saw much of *anything*."

Nancy spotted one of the other security staff, speaking into a walkie-talkie. She rushed over to him and asked where the fire was located.

"I really don't know," he responded. "There are still a few guards inside, and none of them has found the flames."

Nancy quickly repeated this information to George and Bess.

"I came down from the top floor, and there was nothing wrong up there," George commented.

"The top floor," Nancy said slowly. "The furs and jewelry." She didn't tell her friends what she was thinking. Instead she said, "I need to find a phone, quick."

"There's one on the corner," George said. "I saw it when we were chasing those boys."

"Let's go," Nancy said.

When they reached the phone, Nancy quickly inserted some change and dialed Omni Aviation.

"Trish? It's Nancy."

"Nancy!" Trish Jenner sounded excited. "I was hoping you'd call."

"Any news?" Nancy asked.

"Yes," Trish said breathlessly. "Our helicopter pilot is on his way right now. The pickup is five minutes from now."

"Now?" Nancy was surprised. "I thought it was set for tonight. Where is the pickup point?"

"You're not going to believe this," Trish said. "The helicopter is on its way to the roof of Danner and Bishop!"

"Thanks a million, Trish!" Nancy said triumphantly. "You may have just saved the store."

"But, Nancy, what—" Trish was still talking when Nancy shouted "Goodbye" and hung up.

"Come on," she said, turning to Bess and George. "We've got to stop a robbery."

"Back into the store?" Bess wailed as the three of them pushed their way past the crowds on the sidewalk. "I'm not doing it."

"Calm down, Bess," Nancy said. "I'm almost positive there isn't a fire. The smoke is just a diversion to get people out of the store. And with the security staff gone, Danner and Bishop is defenseless."

"Well, okay," Bess said reluctantly, not wanting to let her friends down.

The girls dashed back into the store and grabbed scarves from the accessories counter.

The scarves had been dampened by the water from the sprinklers. Holding the scarves over their mouths and noses, they pushed their way through the smoke-filled aisles toward the escalators.

"These scarves make it easier to breathe," George said in a muffled voice. "But my eyes are watering so much I can hardly see."

"I know," Nancy said sympathetically. "But just keep moving. Maybe the smoke has thinned out on the upper floors."

The escalators weren't running, so the girls raced up the metal stairs as fast as they could.

"It's so quiet," George said as they ran. "Everybody must have fallen for the diversion and left the store."

"Are you sure there isn't really a fire, Nancy?" Bess asked, panting.

Nancy knew her theory about the smoke made sense, but how could she be absolutely sure? She shuddered slightly. If she was wrong, she could be leading her friends straight into a raging fire. It was a huge risk, one she hoped she wouldn't regret.

"Don't think about it, Bess," Nancy said as she bounded up the stairs.

When they reached the top floor, it was just as George had said—there was no trace of smoke or fire. The quiet was eerie.

"Where are we going, anyway?" Bess whispered as the girls moved slowly through the department.

Nancy stopped and stood still for a moment. The girls felt a slight breeze of icy air. Nancy turned to see where the breeze was coming from and spotted a door slightly open. She headed toward the door, Bess and George following close behind.

Nancy looked through a door and saw a stairway leading up to the rooftop. The door on the roof was open, revealing a patch of bright blue sky and the sounds of a loud motor—a helicopter motor.

"Let's check out the rest of this floor," Nancy said in a hushed whisper. "I have a feeling we're not alone up here."

The girls walked as quietly as possible, keeping close to the walls and hiding behind displays so as not to be seen.

Suddenly Nancy stopped and motioned to Bess and George to do the same. Standing as still and quiet as she could, Nancy nodded toward the vault.

The girls saw Nick Holt emptying coats into large boxes. Lindy Dixon was standing behind him, dumping open jewelry cases into a leather valise.

Nancy turned her head and, as calmly as she could, whispered to her friends, "Make a run for a phone and call the police."

"Will do," George whispered back.

But before any of them could act, a familiar voice behind them said, "Don't move a muscle, ladies. I've got a gun, and it's pointed right at you!"

"Mr. Lloyd!" Bess gasped in amazement.

Nick and Lindy looked up from their work.

"How did they get in here?" Nick asked Bennett Lloyd in a surprised voice.

"Don't worry, Nick, I've got them covered," Bennett Lloyd assured him.

"You'll never get away with this," Nancy said quietly. "We know there was no real fire, and so will the Chicago Fire Department. Once they know, the police will be after you!"

"I don't think so," Bennett Lloyd said smoothly. "We put out enough of a smokescreen to fool everyone for quite a while. Either way, we have a helicopter waiting upstairs to make sure of our getaway."

"So all three of you are responsible for the pranks," George said. "We should have known."

"Oh, come on now," Lindy said in a bored voice. She dropped a couple of gold bracelets into the valise. "How could you kids figure out a tricky plot like ours?"

"That's enough chattering," Bennett Lloyd snapped. "Up on the roof, you three."

The girls didn't move.

"Now!" Bennett Lloyd said menacingly.

Slowly the girls started toward the stairs. Nick and Lindy followed close behind them with their bags and boxes of valuables.

On the roof, gusts of cold air flapped at the girls. The Omni helicopter was on the top of the building, its rotor spinning. Nancy realized that Bennett Lloyd was right—the chopper was the perfect escape vehicle for this criminal caper.

"The joker's final prank," Nancy observed, staring coldly at Bennett Lloyd.

"Oh, I have a few more in mind," he said slyly. He motioned to the girls to walk to the edge of the roof. "While Nick and Lindy load the helicopter, let's step over here."

Nancy felt a stab of terror. She had a horrible feeling that Bennett Lloyd was planning to get rid of them—permanently!

"Keep moving," Mr. Lloyd said.

The girls were pushed against the low rail at the edge of the rooftop. Nancy looked over the edge and saw the crowd gathered on the ground below—far below.

Screaming wouldn't help them now, Nancy knew. No one would hear them over the roar of the helicopter. And besides, the people on the sidewalk were too far away to be able to help them. She could only hope that Carlin and Ann Fitzhugh had become suspicious about the fire and had called the police.

Nancy glanced at Bennett Lloyd. There was a

hard look in his eyes that she'd never seen before. She knew he was serious and would stop at nothing to get away.

Bess reached out and grabbed Nancy's arm tightly. "What's he going to do?" Bess asked, her voice quivering with fear.

"I don't know," Nancy answered her friend honestly. Then she turned back to Bennett Lloyd and stared in shock.

His gun was cocked and aimed directly at her!

14

Flight of Fear

Nancy, George, and Bess stood poised on the edge of the rooftop. Bennett Lloyd could give them just one sharp push and they'd fall to their deaths. Or he could use his gun.

"Don't worry," Nancy assured her friends. "He wouldn't dare hurt us."

"Don't try acting brave with me, Nancy Drew," Bennett Lloyd said, moving closer to the girls.

"I'm not acting," Nancy countered. She knew she had to stall him. "I know you don't want to hurt us, Mr. Lloyd."

She was thinking fast, trying to come up with a plan. Nancy hoped that Bennett Lloyd was not an experienced gunman. If I can just manage a way to catch him off guard, Nancy thought.

But he was staring steadily at the girls. It was clear to Nancy that he wasn't about to let his guard down for a second.

"I'm sick of your meddling," Bennett Lloyd said to Nancy. "I've been wanting to get rid of you ever since you showed up at this store. You've been nothing but trouble, sticking your nose into things that are none of your business. Well, now I can—"

Suddenly a huge, strong blast of water came shooting out of nowhere. The powerful spray hit Bennett Lloyd in the side, forcing him to stumble and fall to the ground. His gun flew out of his hands and lodged itself in an air vent.

The girls quickly ran away from the edge of the roof. Nancy tried to see where the water was coming from. She caught her breath when she saw who it was.

It was Joe Dane! He stood there, larger than life, holding one of the fire hoses that had been coiled up on the roof.

Nancy and her friends dashed over to where Joe was standing. He was wearing big smile on his face as he sprayed Bennett Lloyd full force.

"They had me tied up and locked in a closet," Joe told Nancy. "But I finally got out. I still know a few tricks from my days on the force."

Nick and Lindy saw what was happening and sprang into action. They rushed toward Joe to try to get the fire hose away from him. Joe turned the powerful hose spray on Nick, stopping him in his tracks.

Lindy tried to attack Joe from another angle. But before she could get near him, Bess crept up behind her and gave her former boss a solid push. Lindy went sprawling down on the dirty surface of the rooftop. Before Lindy could get up, Bess was on her, pinning her to the ground.

"Bess, is that you?" George asked in amazement. She had never seen her cousin do anything like that before.

Nancy said, "You'd better go for the police, George."

"I'm on my way," George said with a nod.

But while Joe had the hose pointed at Nick Holt, Bennett Lloyd had gotten to his feet. He yanked his gun from the vent and grabbed George, sticking the cold nose of the weapon in her back. George was his hostage.

Bennett Lloyd shouted over the roar of the helicopter rotors and the rush of hose water.

"Put that hose down," he screamed to Joe Dane. "I'm warning you!"

"And you two, back off!" He gestured at Bess, who immediately released Lindy.

Nancy's heart sank as she looked at Bennett

Lloyd. His eyes were wild with desperation. Nancy knew she couldn't take any chances. George's life was at stake!

"Joe," Nancy called out, signaling wildly. "Please drop the hose, as he says."

Joe saw that he he had no choice. He reluctantly dropped the hose. The water spray had been their last hope.

Lloyd dragged George with him across the rooftop, then directed her to get into the waiting helicopter.

"And you two," he yelled at Nick and Lindy, who were still sprawled on the rooftop floor, "get up! Finish stashing the things into the chopper. Let's go, move it!"

For the first time, Nancy noticed the helicopter pilot. The poor man was roped to his seat, his wrists and ankles tied together. His face reflected the anger of a hostage.

Nick Holt got up off the wet ground and pulled a gun out from under his jacket. He pointed it at the pilot.

"Stay right where you are," Nick ordered as he untied the ropes around the pilot's limbs. "If you want to live, you'll fly this chopper where we want to go."

The pilot glared at Nick. He settled back angrily, unable to argue with the gun pointed at him.

Nancy watched with a sinking heart as Bennett

Lloyd pushed George into the helicopter. Lindy and Nick followed with the last of their bags of stolen Danner and Bishop merchandise.

Nancy's mind raced. What was she going to do? She couldn't let George be kidnapped.

When the helicopter door closed with a sharp clang, Nancy sprinted forward. She grabbed the fire hose in the hope that she could knock out the helicopter's electrical system.

But the roof was slippery from the water that had been sprayed. Nancy lost her footing just as she got close enough to the helicopter. She fell to the ground with a thud.

The helicopter was already taking off. The noise was deafening. In addition to the constant whirring of the main rotor blades, the small tail rotor blades were beating the air with a high frequency.

The helicopter was going to disappear with George! And no one knew where the chopper was headed.

Nancy knew she had no time to think of a plan. In desperation, she grabbed hold of the landing skid at the bottom of the chopper, as if she hoped to pull it back.

The helicopter continued to rise—with Nancy clinging to the landing skid!

In her desperation to save her friend, she clutched the skid with all her might as the machine lifted her farther up into the air. The helicopter cleared the roof of Danner and Bishop. Nancy looked down and saw the crowds of onlookers below. She was several hundred feet above the ground.

Nancy tried to think clearly. But one thought dominated. Any second she might lose her grip and fall to the street below—to certain death. Nancy was terrified. But she had to keep her head—*and* keep the strength in her arms!

She was being blasted with powerful gusts of air from the overhead rotor blades. Nancy knew she wouldn't be able to hold on that way much longer. Her arms were starting to give out, and the steady blast of air pushing against her was weakening her quickly.

Slowly and carefully, she tried to maneuver herself under the fuselage. If she could get directly under the center of the helicopter body, it might shield her a little from the destructive downwash.

Nancy glanced upward to look for a better place to hold on. The powerful wind almost blinded her, and the pain in her hands was getting worse.

She realized that her fingers were beginning to freeze.

Nancy tried to get her legs up around the skid, but the air blasts were working against her. In desperation, she began swinging like a gymnast on the high bar.

Suddenly it paid off! On the high part of her swing, she caught her foot on a metal handle.

Nancy struggled and managed to climb up directly under the helicopter body. She grasped a couple of metal handles tightly.

Now she was shielded from the downwash wind and hidden from the view of the kidnappers above.

But Nancy's heart twisted with fear. She had to face the facts. No one except the crooks knew where the helicopter was headed. How would the police be able to follow them to rescue George and herself?

Nancy was almost paralyzed by the cold. She was being buffeted by savage winds that were unbelievably strong up there in the sky. But she held on.

You can make it. Just don't let go, she told herself. She shut her eyes tightly against the stinging wind.

A little later, after the pain had subsided, she opened her eyes so she could see where they were going. She looked down.

Below her were church spires, wintry-bare treetops, warehouses, and the tall buildings of Chicago. It was all laid out before her like a toy city around a child's electric train set.

The helicopter descended slightly, turned, and headed for the Chicago River. Oh, great, Nancy thought. Was the helicopter going to land on some kind of boat?

Nancy allowed her eyes to travel downward to the streets below, and she was sure she glimpsed the blinking lights of police cars. The cars were snaking along the streets. It seemed as if the police were trying to follow the helicopter.

An ambulance was rapidly following the police cars. Nancy could barely see the white van with its red markings and its revolving light. And it made a chill settle in around Nancy's heart.

Nancy realized grimly that the ambulance was for her.

I have news for them, she thought with fierce determination. I have no intention of letting go.

Suddenly one end of the metal handles cracked in her hand. Nancy tightened her grip, but she suspected that it would be only a matter of seconds before the other handle broke off, too. And there was nothing else she could hold on to.

Nancy looked up and noticed that there was a small square of metal with no rivet fasteners around its edge. It looked big enough for both of her hands. She also saw a small lever on one side of the panel. Could this be some kind of opening into the helicopter? Nancy wondered.

With her free hand, Nancy pried the lever, and the small hatch opened. She thrust her hand into the hole and gripped the edge just as the handle in her other hand broke free.

The hatch opening was warmer, and Nancy knew it must be connected to the engine compartment.

The warmth felt good on her hands, but unfortunately the metal also had oil dripped on it. The slippery oil made if difficult to hang on, so Nancy had to tighten her grip even more. She could feel the muscles in her forearms straining.

The helicopter was over the river now and dipping in altitude. Nancy wondered whether the police were trailing them by radar. As long as they flew high above the treetops, the helicopter would show up on radar scanners. If they flew low over the river, though, the police might lose track of them.

Nancy had a clear view of freighters and barges sailing up the river.

The choppy water sparkled and gleamed, a deep, cold blue. Sometimes it glinted like shards of ice, as though parts of it were frozen.

Nancy realized that the helicopter was now about seventy feet above the river. She scanned the area, looking for a clue to where the helicopter might be heading.

Then she spotted a large flat boat sitting motionless in the water. The barge had a big white circle drawn on its surface. The circle looked like a bull's-eye on a dartboard.

It was a helipad.

That had to be it! Bennett Lloyd and his fellow

criminals must have rented the boat to make their final escape.

The helicopter was dipping lower, and Nancy realized that she was heading for big trouble.

She knew that she had to jump. If the criminals saw her, they would capture her. She wouldn't be able to save George if she were being held hostage, too. She had to make her move now, while she was still able to.

She took a couple of deep breaths to gather her courage for her next move. Nancy would have to dive before the helicopter was over the barge. Yet she was still far enough above the river that the plunge would be extremely dangerous.

Nancy waited until the last possible moment.

Then she closed her eyes and released her grip on the engine compartment hatch. Her head slammed against the right landing skid as she started her fall.

Nancy felt herself blacking out as she dropped, out of control, toward the water!

15

The Joker Speaks

Nancy hit the river just before she lost consciousness, and the icy cold water sprang her into action. She was a powerful swimmer and began immediately to kick hard, propelling herself upward.

In no time, she had her head out of the water and was taking long, deep breaths of air.

Bobbing around in the choppy water, Nancy felt her teeth begin to chatter. She couldn't remember ever having been this cold before.

She knew that such cold water was treacherous. If Nancy didn't keep moving, she could freeze. She also had to keep moving to avoid being pulled down by the river's undertow.

Nancy kept her arms and legs moving rapidly

in the freezing river water. She tried to think of something besides the cold.

She had to figure out a way to rescue George from those criminals!

While Nancy watched the helicopter land on the boat, she wondered whether Bennett Lloyd would let the pilot or George go free. With a shudder, she remembered the wild look in Mr. Lloyd's eyes back on the Danner and Bishop roof. He was desperate enough to want to get rid of everyone.

As she was thinking of Bennett Lloyd, he climbed out of the helicopter. She was close enough to see that his face was red with excitement.

George stepped out of the helicopter. The winter winds whipped at her dark curls. George looked calm, but Nancy knew that her friend was covering up her fear.

Lindy and Nick came next, hauling the bags of jewelry and furs they had stolen from Danner and Bishop. Nancy tried to keep her hopes from sinking.

She kept her mind on the only one small advantage that she had: the criminals didn't know that she was nearby in the water.

Nancy was glad to see the helicopter take off in a hurry as soon as all of the bags and boxes had been unloaded. At least they had let the pilot go.

Nancy realized that she was tiring quickly from

the icy cold water and the helicopter ride. If she didn't think of something soon, it would be too late.

Just then, George looked down into the river. She spotted Nancy at once, and her mouth fell open with shock. George gulped hard but never let her captors suspect what was floating in the Chicago River near them.

Good work, George, Nancy thought gratefully.

Nancy knew she had to get out of the freezing water soon. She wondered if she could climb up the side of the barge. She glided closer to the barge and searched for a place to grab on.

"What's that?" demanded Bennett Lloyd. "I heard something!"

"Just your nerves, Bennett," Lindy Dixon told him.

"I don't think so. I think there's someone in the water!"

Nancy flattened herself against the side of the barge. Her heart was pounding against her chest. If Bennett Lloyd saw her, she knew it would be the end. He would shoot her, and then there would be no one to save George.

"Well, I don't see anything," Bennett Lloyd admitted after a long pause.

"I do!" Nick Holt suddenly exclaimed. "Look over there!"

"What is that?" Lindy asked, peering into the distance.

"It looks like a Coast Guard cruiser," said Nick.

The Coast Guard! Nancy wanted to cheer. Help was on the way.

"We've got to get out of here," Bennett Lloyd announced. "How do we get this thing moving?"

"I'll get us going," Nick said.

But there wasn't enough time for Nick to take action. The Coast Guard cruiser was already approaching the barge. A voice booming over a public address system was warning the crew not to move.

When the cruiser was alongside the barge, six officers jumped onto the barge. Nancy pushed away from the hull a bit so that she could see what was happening. The officers surrounded the three criminals.

"Drop the guns," one of the officers ordered. Nancy saw Nick Holt drop his weapon with no argument. She could tell that he was scared.

Bennett Lloyd wasn't quite so willing, though. His gun was pointed at George's back. "Get back," he yelled at the Coast Guard officers. "Get back, or I'll kill her." His hand started to shake as he moved closer to George.

It was a standoff, and any minute Bennett Lloyd might panic. Nancy knew she had to do something.

Then she spotted some of the ship's towing line dangling in the water. Quickly she swam over, grabbed one of the ropes, and slowly pulled herself on board.

Nancy's positioning was perfect. She had come up only a few feet behind Bennett Lloyd. A few of the Coast Guard officers saw her but made no move to give her away.

Cautiously, Nancy began inching forward. She could see that the store manager was getting more and more nervous. He was looking for a way out and trying to keep track of all the Coast Guard officers. Nancy was afraid that he would see her before she could grab him.

Just then, a woman officer deliberately shifted her position to distract Bennett Lloyd. As he snapped his gun in her direction, Nancy made her move. She kicked the gun from his hand and threw her arm around his neck.

Within seconds, he was seized and handcuffed by several officers. Nancy let go and turned to see the relief written on George's face.

The Coast Guard officers frisked Bennett Lloyd, Nick, and Lindy. Nancy watched as the criminals were handcuffed and led onto the Coast Guard cruiser.

"Are you all right?" one of the officers asked Nancy. Another threw a blanket over her shoulders.

"I'm fine," Nancy assured them through chattering teeth.

"Let's get you back to our cruiser," said

the first officer. "You'll need dry clothes right away!"

George hurried over to give her friend a big hug, even though Nancy was dripping wet.

"How in the world did you get here, Nan?" George asked.

"The same way you got here," Nancy replied. "But I had to hang on to the outside of the helicopter!"

"Nancy, you really outdid yourself this time!" George said, grinning.

"What I want to know is how the Coast Guard found this barge," Nancy said, turning to the Coast Guard captain.

"We got a phone call from a Ms. Trish Jenner, from Omni Aviation," the captain told her. "She wasn't sure what was going on, but she knew something was up. She was worried about you. She also knew the drop-off site of those passengers was going to be here on this boat in the river, so she asked us to check it out. Then, on our way here, we got a call from the police."

Nancy grinned happily. "Trish was a big help, but I never dreamed that she'd turn out to be this good a friend!

"We're going to have to treat Trish to a great dinner," Nancy said to George. By then, Nancy's lips were turning blue from the cold. One of the officers noticed and said, "Come on, girls. We've got more blankets on the cruiser, so you can warm up. We'll take you back to the dock."

When they had reached the Coast Guard dock, they found the Fitzhughs waiting, along with Bess and Joe Dane.

As soon as she saw her friends, Bess ran to hug them. "I was *so* worried!" She cried. "Nancy, I couldn't believe it when I saw you hanging on to that helicopter."

After reassuring everyone that they were fine, the two girls told them what had happened.

When they were finished, two police cars drove up. The Coast Guard officers started to turn the prisoners over to the police officers.

"Just one minute," Carlin Fitzhugh said in his commanding voice. "I'd like to talk to Bennett Lloyd first." He stepped over to the little man.

"I've got to know, Bennett," Carlin Fitzhugh said. "After all our years together—why would you get involved with something like this?"

Bennett Lloyd was eager to talk. He held his head high, and his pale gray eyes flashed with a sharp, unmistakable bitterness.

"I'll tell you why," he said, almost stumbling over his words. "In all my thirty years with Danner and Bishop, you never appreciated my loyalty, Carlin."

"But that's ridiculous," Mr. Fitzhugh stated, his face turning red with outrage.

"Is it?" Bennett Lloyd asked smoothly. "You only appreciated people who were *family*, like Joe Dane and your other relatives!"

"Well . . ." Carlin Fitzhugh looked confused. "Well, of course, family always comes first, that's my motto, but—"

"But nothing," Bennett Lloyd spat out. "I always knew where I stood: *nowhere.* Your daughter, Ann, has come in now to take over, and that was the final straw. Old Lloyd would have been out on the garbage heap!"

"Never!" Ann Fitzhugh protested.

"Oh, yes." Bennett Lloyd's face was grim and determined. "There would have been no more advancement for me. For all I've done to build Danner and Bishop, I've gotten nothing in return—not even a decent salary. So I took what I felt was owed me. In *merchandise.*"

"That's crazy," Carlin Fitzhugh said, shaking his head. "Just crazy."

"At least I made *you* crazy, too," Bennett Lloyd said with satisfaction. "I designed those joker cards myself, you know. You know what a joker is, don't you? A fool, a loyal servant in the king's court—just like me!" Bennett Lloyd sounded proud of his cleverness.

"You played me for a fool, Carlin. But my cards showed that even a fool can strike back!"

Nancy thought back to all the terrible practical

jokes and realized how Bennett Lloyd must have enjoyed watching everyone, especially the Fitzhughs, squirming and worrying.

"But what about these two?" George asked curiously, pointing to Lindy Dixon and Nick Holt. She turned to them. "Why did you do it?"

Lindy and Nick weren't talking, so Nancy told the group her theory.

"Nick probably did it partly for the money," Nancy said. "But I imagine he wanted some excitement in his life, too."

"It sure beat scrubbing floors!" Nick said, a wicked grin on his face. "You can thank me for the escalator ride and the falling lighting fixture. Too bad you survived!"

"And Lindy, I'll bet, did it purely for the money," Nancy went on. "She wanted to get a nice big bank account so she could head to New York to become an actress. Working in the shoe department just didn't pay enough. Am I right, Lindy?"

"Of course. I'm a good actress," Lindy said in a haughty voice. "And I'll make a terrific star."

"I'm sure you will," Bess told her sweetly. "You'll have plenty of time to star—in court and in prison!"

"You said it, Bess!" George agreed as Lindy and the other two were led away by the Chicago police.

"But what about you, Joe?" Nancy turned to Joe Dane. "How did they overpower a big guy like you?"

The big man looked embarrassed. "Last night Nick showed up at my house and caught me off guard. He jumped me and knocked me out. When I woke up, I was tied up and locked in a broom closet at the store."

"Why did they do that to you?" George asked.

Joe Dane shrugged. "They were afraid I knew too much, I guess. They were planning to take me along as a hostage, then get rid of me. But then they grabbed George instead."

"It was lucky for us that you were out of that broom closet in time to spray them with that fire hose," Nancy reminded him. "Otherwise, Bennett Lloyd would have finished us off."

"I was glad to help," Joe said, smiling. Nancy smiled, too. Joe had turned out to be a big help in solving the mystery.

A little later, the whole group was seated around the dining table of the Fitzhugh mansion, enjoying a hearty meal. Everyone in the party looked relieved. The ordeal was finally over.

"I've been trying to think how to thank you three girls—and Joe," Carlin Fitzhugh said. "Ann has just suggested a way." He paused a moment for effect.

Then he said, "I want you all to have a free shopping spree, courtesy of Danner and Bishop!"

"Hey, that's great!" Bess was the first to react.

"All *right*," George said with a huge grin.

"You deserve it," Ann Fitzhugh told them.

"It's very generous of you," Nancy said, smiling. "But what I want to know is—is Bess going to start with the shoe department?"

Bess waved her hands.

"I never want to see another shoe as long as I live," she declared dramatically.

"Remember, folks," George said teasingly. "You heard it here first."

"So Bess is finally cured of her shoe obsession," Nancy said, trying to keep a straight face.

Bess suddenly looked alarmed. "You didn't *really* believe me, did you?" she asked quickly. "There's room in my closet for at least another twenty pairs!" She smiled. "And that's no joke!"

THE HARDY BOYS® SERIES
By Franklin W. Dixon